SQUATCH WATCH

SQUATCH WATCH

Sharan Mason Nelson

This book is
dedicated to supportive friends who advised,
encouraged and trusted that I could get this project
completed. Special thanks to Nancy Ward, Anita Gorglione,
Christy Johnson, and Lee Race for being my great source of motivation,
and especially for your invaluable feedback.

Squatch Watch Mountain

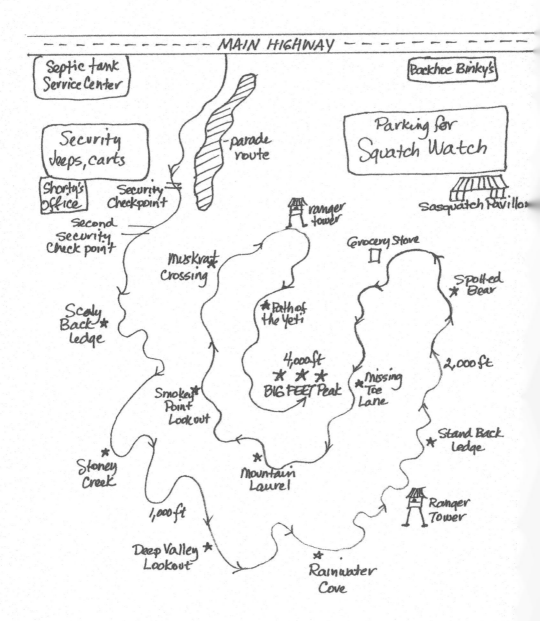

CAST OF CHARACTERS

Shorty Tubbottom
Owner of Bigfeet Peak and the park called Squatch Watch.

Mountain Men Hunters
Franklin, Bubba, Jimbo
All grew up hunting and fishing and loving the mountain life.

U. S. Professional Bigfoot Hunters
Clarice
A primatologist, scientist who is skeptical about
Bigfoot, but always in the hunt.
Clive
Scientist that believes Bigfoot exists and has spent
most of his life in the hunt for Bigfoot.
Matthew
Scientist and fellow believer, uses his giant lungs
for calling Bigfoot.

The College Professors
Rhonda, Denise, Lulu
All out of their element but here to support their belief that
there is no such thing as a Bigfoot, Yeti or Sasquatch.

Andrew
Shorty Tubbottom's right hand man, his spy, cook
for the hunters

Chapter 1
Shorty's Dream

Franklin thought it strange that the woman was stuffing hot chocolate packets into her blouse. Tall and slender, she appeared elegantly refined in a long, metallic vest over a soft, silky blouse, a black pencil skirt and gold shiny sandals. Even her toenails sparkled! She did not look like any Bigfoot hunter he had ever seen. Franklin's attention went back to the gathering of Yeti hunters and the speaker, Mr. Shorty Tubbottom, the extremely proud owner of Squatch Watch Park.

"Most think folktales are made-up stories or untruths. But folk-tales are based on the experience of a culture, actual happenings that are passed down through the generations. I grew up hearing about Sasquatch and the many people who'd witnessed the reign of the Bigfoot on *this very mountain*. Every family reunion, as far back as I can remember, was centered around the tales of Bigfoot. A few were tales of terror but most were just simple sightings. I, myself, actually believe the nocturnal Sasquatch to be timid, even mild mannered. Sasquatch picked the perfect sanctuary for himself and his family."

The ten hunters looked at each other in disbelief. Anyone with a lick of sense would know it is not wise to underestimate a monster. To them, Bigfoot would never go gently in the night. But their job was to find out. They were here to capture the cryptid, to prove his existence.

"My plan is for you to capture Bigfoot. We will show the world that Bigfoot is just like goats or cows or pigs, docile and even obedient. Yes! We will capture Bigfoot and build a habitat where people from all over the world can come and see how Bigfoot lives, mates and has managed to endure, for centuries, without the help of humans. I am *more than certain* that a flurry of yetis live on this mountain."

Coming from a wealthy background, some would say that Shorty Tubbottom had more money than sense. This just might be his "Disney-land," but without the cartoon characters. He, and he alone, owns Squatch Watch Park and now the world would know him better than Walt Disney. Soon his mountain would be the new home of the myth, the legend, Bigfoot, with millions of people coming to see, study and even taunt the family of Bigfoot living on his green mound. Oh yes, Shorty Tubbottom knew his fate, and it felt exciting. Shorty's destiny was here and now. *Come see the greatest show on earth, the most hunted on earth, the most elusive on earth: Sasquatch!*

His mother worried constantly about Shorty. He was not well liked as a child, nor as an adult. As a youngster, he badgered other children until he got his way, and then would turn around and call them names for giving in. "Sissy. Wimp. Lucy the Loser." In adulthood, he found out that other men would not put up with this, and had his butt kicked a few times.

Whenever she could, she would do anything to boost his self-esteem. She even signed over her inheritance; the $100 million dollar piece of property now known as Squatch Watch. Shorty had begged and pleaded and hurled himself down on the couch a thousand times before Mama Tubbottom finally gave in, too tired to resist his petitions any more. She signed away her mountain to her beloved son with high hopes they would all be sitting pretty in the next few years. All of her family's fortune, and now her life savings, were going towards placating Shorty. The family fortune was now tied up in a mountain for big, hairy dinosaurs—or something like that—she was not very clear. She was clear, however, that he was happy for the first time in a very long time. She liked seeing him like that; confident and assured. He had finally found something to focus his attention on, something worthwhile "for all mankind," he said. No mother was ever more proud of her big, all grown up son, who was one inch taller than her five feet.

Now, a new beginning for Shorty was underway *and* for Mama Tubbottom. She was going to be the 'Queen of the Mountain,' as Shorty put it, and there would be parades and celebrations, and millions of people would see Sasquatch in its natural habitat.

Shorty continued his presentation to the hunters. "Eventually, the whole mountain is to be used to house Bigfoot and its tribe. It is fourteen miles up the mountain with its twists and turns. Elevation is right at 4,000 feet. There are barricades and large fences at the lowest elevation to keep Bigfoot from escaping. The fence is manned by a highly trained security squad, well camouflaged and hidden. Electric fences and floodlights ring the perimeter with a large parking area for the visitors and RVs. You saw that when you came in."

However, Shorty neglected to tell the hunters that security had seen no Bigfoot. Rangers had seen no Bigfoot. Cherokee scouts had seen no Bigfoot. Satellites had photographed no Bigfoot. Shorty knew they were here, though. His family had promised it so, with all the stories and sightings. Now he must hire this new crew to capture the cagey Sasquatch for display.

With nothing left to do, Shorty had sent out an inquiry with a huge reward for the capture of his Bigfoot creatures that are certainly living on his mountain. No harm should befall them. Shorty needed the creature(s) to be well and active. NO LETHAL WEAPONS ALLOWED anywhere in the park. Large signs displayed this message at the entrance. Only bear spray would be permitted. Shorty explained he would like to house the creature in a certain area with dugouts showing Bigfoot in its sleeping habitat, Bigfoot devouring large chunks of fresh meat, Bigfoot swimming in a man-made grotto. At that moment, and if one looked closely, dollar signs could be seen in Shorty's eyes as he conjured up the home of Bigfoot. How else was he to repay his Mama? Yes, they will be 'King and Queen of Squatch Watch Park!'

Near an old dilapidated restaurant and just beyond Elmer's Septic and Sewer Service, but before Backhoe Binky's, was the turn for the big Squatch Watch Park. Driving in, parking was on the left and security was ahead on the right. So much was at stake, keeping Bigfoot alive and well in the park. There were no accommodations as of yet but the parking lot indicated that Shorty Tubbottom was expecting a gigantic crowd to descend upon his beloved home.

Tonight, only security, Shorty Tubbottom, catering staff and the hunters were gathered at one end of the parking lot, under Sasquatch Pavilion, decked out with iced sodas, bottled water, paper plates and napkins, along with plastic flatware. There was a large barbecue pit, releasing smoke into the dusky evening sky, filling the air with succulent roast pig. *Certainly Bigfoot would come to see and smell what this party was all about.* The side tables were loaded with pickles, olives, chips and breads and all kinds of chilled salads, from coleslaw to pasta salad and lobster rolls. Further into the flat, open area, there was a bonfire surrounded by benches. On a table there was a coffee urn, with cream and sugar, and all the makings for s'mores, including long-handled forks for use in the bonfire.

Everyone gravitated to the aroma of the delicious food. Shorty instructed them all to help themselves and then be seated, so that he could continue his introduction to the park.

"Enjoy your last supper!" Shorty teased them. "We won't be offering food like this again. Well, we will see what you accomplish and *then* decide." Everyone clapped and turned their attention back to the food. "You can purchase snacks and protein bars from the rangers, but no food will be kept out, since bears, raccoons and opossums would enjoy that service. Whatever food you have with you, be sure to guard it with your life."

Everyone ate their fill. The female professors were the only ones who thought to confiscate as much food as they could, hidden in napkins, purses, and pockets to keep in the camper's fridge. Rhonda whispered, "Hey, they could feed fifty more people and still not run out of food! Pack some away for later." And she proceeded to snatch a lobster roll, a jumbo barbecue sandwich, hidden in her purse, along with graham crackers and chocolate bars stuffed in every pocket. She even hid hot chocolate packets, tucking them in her blouse.

Shorty Tubbottom welcomed the professional hunters to the park. He explained his objectives: 1) Capturing at least two of the creatures, 2) Enclosing the park with security and armed guards, and 3) Displaying the daily habits of Bigfoot, with viewing areas for his visitor's enjoyment. He thought it was important to learn all that we could from Bigfoot, for it seems to have outsmarted humankind for a very long time now.

The hunters wanted to know about the reward. Shorty explained that he wanted the creatures to be found unharmed. They could use any kind of trap, snare or pit to capture Bigfoot. He had explained all of this in their informational packets. The hunt, reward, and the expectations were outlined when they were first notified about this massive project. Many hunters were interviewed and reported what kind of measures they would use in the capture of Bigfoot. There were some novel ideas. All of the applicants had then been whittled down by picking the different means by which Bigfoot could be captured with optimal success. Certainly, the million dollar reward was incentive enough to accomplish this goal. Shorty planned to pay the reward by selling tickets, making a movie about the capture or even creating a traveling show, whatever it took. It was clear, from the beginning, that no weapons were allowed. The hunters must use their wits, their experience, their talents to find and contain the creature. They could use snares, cages, hoists, traps, even slingshots if that helped. The stakes were sky high. Shorty didn't care if the reward went to one individual or to a group. The capture was all that mattered. If they captured only one, that was quite alright, for the other cryptids would find their way to the captured one. Shorty was certain of that.

A hand went up in the aromatic air and Shorty motioned for the hunter to ask his question. In reply, out came a large map, placed on an easel, and a long pointer was handed to Shorty. It was a map of his mountain.

"It's a long trek up the mountain to the peak. In the foothills, you will come across many markers with names, such as Scaly Back Ledge and Stoney Creek. At 1,000 feet, you'll come across Deep Valley Lookout—a lovely spot—and then move on to Rain Water Cove, where a ranger tower is constantly manned and monitored for sightings. Up the mountain, at the 2,000 foot marker is Stand Back Ledge, a narrow and dangerous curve for RVs and campers." He pointed to the ledge. "Please. Please. Please proceed with caution here." He warned.

No longer listening, Franklin glanced at the tall professor, wondering what would make a sophisticated lady like her want to be a part of this dirty, messy hunt.

"The next marker is called Spotted Bear which is near the small grocery store. There you'll find snacks, ice cream and hot coffee–for you, and then later for the crowds that will be traveling these paths." (Shorty was always optimistic.) Shorty moved in closer to the large map and with a smile, he gestured to a spot.

"This is Missing Toe Lane. No one knows how it got its name but you can use your imagination. On around the bend, we come to Mountain Laurel, a beautiful spot for those on the way up, especially in the early spring of the year. Nearing the 3,000 foot mark is Smokey Point Lookout. This is another expansive view of the lush valley below. Here, too, are the narrow springs of the creek from up above, with a waterfall trickling down the sloping, mossy mountainside. This mountain is thick with woods and abundant wildlife." Shorty bragged about the bountiful beauty here on his mound of earth.

"Since there is no cell service, you need to remember these markers. It will help the rangers find you. One of the last markers of the mountain is Muskrat Crossing. It's a smelly spot on the way to the top, mainly during spring, when the muskrats, deer and cats mark their territories. They do this in hopes of finding a mate." Shorty embraced the pointer as if embracing a new love, his head and eyes tilted heavenward. Most everyone laughed at his swooning body, all but Andrew, Shorty's spy, who was ready to get this hunt underway.

"I have a little more to share with you," he said, noticing people were getting anxious to get to the bonfire and the s'mores. "There is one more ranger tower near the top. The ever-vigilant rangers spend hours watching and waiting, hoping and praying Bigfoot will stumble out of the brush surrounding the tower. The rangers have binocular rings permanently pressed around their eyes, ever-hopeful for the creature to step into view. The rangers are also on alert to any kind of aircraft near the mountain, be it a small plane or a helicopter getting too close. They are a superior group of professionals and are here to help. But they will stay out of your way. Just a reminder," Shorty held his hand high, to emphasize this important fact, waving it as he continued, "the rangers must be contacted immediately upon a capture of Bigfoot. They will 'dart' the creature and transport it to the awaiting habitat. Andrew, the camp coordinator, will be able to get in touch by radio with the rangers. Stand up, Andrew, so everyone knows who you are." Andrew barely stood and appeared irritated.

Back to his map, Shorty was close to finishing. "Up next is the 'Path of the Yeti' marker. There is a nice, broad stream that brings coyotes and bears to this feasting spot. Pools of fish linger in the fresh, cool water, unaware of the waiting mountain lions and bobcats that love to feast on them. These hunters will also find rabbits, squirrels, beavers, and even moles coming to satisfy their thirst. Also, among the chain of predators are hawks, eagles, and owls. All of these mountain creatures unknowingly contribute to the tasty, lush environment of Sasquatch!"

With a flourish of the pointer, Shorty eagerly comes to the top of the mountain. "Here, we find the peak. This whole mountain has been scoured for signs of Bigfoot. The price on the head of Bigfoot has become astronomical. It is imperative that he be found now, as quickly as possible. You, dear friends, are here for one purpose only; to snare Bigfoot. And you will have Saturday, Sunday and Monday in which to do it. I wish you all the best of luck. We will see you all on Tuesday morning."

Shorty Tubbottom left the pavilion.

Franklin watched the slender woman, with bulging pockets, join her two female pals and head to the fire pit for s'mores. All three were over-dressed for this hunting expedition. Strange. Certainly, they had more practical clothing, if they were going to participate in this hunt for Bigfoot.

Chapter 2
Ten Little Hunters

Ten hunters moved to the bonfire area. They eyed each other suspiciously. Andrew, the camp cook, broke the silence and asked the group what they thought would be the best way to capture Bigfoot. No one responded right away. Andrew appeared reserved, even angry. He was told he could not participate in the hunt, since he was an employee of Shorty Tubbottom. But he certainly had other plans. That reward was his. He was tired of being Shorty's gopher, his eyes and ears in the field, doing grunt work for other hunters, especially for very little profit. He moved to the fire, stomping his way over to it. That million dollars would build a mighty fine life for him.

Rhonda, the tall, overdressed participant, piped up, "Well, I think the best way to catch the beast is with snares of some type." That was the plan of Rhonda, Denise and Lulu, to use rope snares but really to do as little as possible. They were college professors, and had come, secretly, to prove there was no such thing as Bigfoot. Shorty had invited the professors *(equal opportunity?)* but did not expect much from them. None of the female professors believed in Bigfoot but Shorty didn't know that.

Denise had ventured into the woods, to look and listen to the forest before it got dark. She took time to sit in the undergrowth and contemplate this weekend, hoping to use her scientific eye to gather information for their research. She had never ventured into a forest before. She momentarily felt brave but soon returned to the bonfire to be with friends and, *don't forget,* to have dessert.

Lulu was interested in environmental research; real research in the great outdoors. Something she had not done in her professional career. So here she was, ready to jump into the wild, with both feet, too, as long as there were others beside her.

Andrew never moved his gaze from the marshmallow he was burning in the heat of the bonfire. As he clasped the marshmallow between two crackers, he raised his eyebrows. He seemed to dismiss her idea of rope snares with a wave that appeared to shoo away an annoying gnat.

"Snares are good," Jimbo stepped forward, feeling he needed to rescue the woman. *Oh, if he only knew!* Rhonda never needed to be rescued!

"What's your name, Son?

"Jimbo, Sir."

"Well, Jimbo, snares might work." Andrew took a big bite of the s'more and then continued, "but this is a big fellow we're talkin' bout. Snares would have to be pretty strong and pretty big. I'm thinking you'd have to use something more heavy duty." He shoved the rest of the gooey concoction into his mouth.

"Okay, snares may not be the way to go. Me and my pals here, Bubba, Franklin and myself think Bigfoot can be enticed using smells and food."

"Not bad." Andrew shrugged his shoulders and continued, "I think you're on the right track."

Andrew turned to the other group of hunters seated together. Clive stood up and faced the fire. "We've been hunting Bigfoot for a good number of years and we think using calls, even amplified music would help Bigfoot to come near. I'm Clive and this is my crew. We're members of the U.S.A. Professional Bigfoot Hunters." Clive, Clarice and Matthew all nodded toward Andrew and the others.

Andrew was sizing up the competition. At this point, he was not seeing much, in his opinion. He smiled but said nothing. He shoved another melting treat into his mouth and pointed to his ear.

"Using sound, such as music, is smart, since you are using the sense of hearing. And of course, you constantly use the sense of sight, just as the rangers here at Squatch Watch. Can't really use touch, not until you actually catch a Bigfoot." He rubbed his fingertips together. Then he lifted both index fingers to tap each side of his nose. "This is the most important sense you will need in these woods!" He leered at the hunters menacingly. "YOU WILL SMELL BIGFOOT BEFORE YOU EVER SEE HIM!" His voice boomed in the still night air. Stunned by his bellowing, no one moved a muscle.

Andrew trampled the grass as he went over to a darkened area and pulled out a sleeping bag from his gear. He flattened it out close to the fire. He threw a log onto the bonfire and then settled down on his skimpy bag. He certainly didn't think there was any competition from this group. The others watched as he stretched out. He laughed, and with ominous tones, he repeated, "Just keep sniffing the air. Just keep sniffing the air."

As mentioned, the Bigfoot Hunters would use music, amplifiers, calls, even dancing to entice Bigfoot to come to their campfire. From their experience, they believed Bigfoot to be interested in performances, if only for entertainment purposes. The Bigfoot Hunters would knock on trees and call, yell, scream, and screech as a way to connect and communicate with Bigfoot in its own habitat. Maybe they would even use Clarice and her feminine wiles to persuade him to come a little closer.

Also, there were the Mountain Men Hunters, three young men who grew up in the hills and knew how to scout and track all kinds of critters. They were Bubba, Franklin and Jimbo. Jimbo was the chivalrous fellow who had stood up to protect Rhonda earlier when he thought Andrew was being rude. Franklin had spied Rhonda swiping the food. All three of the Mountain Men were very bashful when it came to women. But they were here to capture Bigfoot, and more importantly to capture the reward, not hearts. They planned to use dead animals or maybe some fruits and chocolates carefully laced with sleeping pills to bring Bigfoot into their traps.

Not believing in Bigfoot but playing the part of hunters, the three female professors, Rhonda, Denise and Lulu, would pretend by using rope snares—nothing too elaborate or time consuming, *since there is no Bigfoot to be caught!* They believed men use the excuse of Bigfoot to spend time in the woods, away from wives and kids, to basically skip responsibilities. Well, that was Rhonda's deep-seated belief and she dragged Denise and Lulu along as comrades in the hunt for the fanciful Bigfoot.

Then there was Andrew. A weird, cocky bird to say the least. He was hired by Shorty to set up a daily camp where he was to cook and feed the hunters. He could hunt and catch, if need be, whatever they needed as far as meals, but only if the coolers ran out of food, which were stowed away under the camper. He was mainly to use his talent of spying—his eyes were Shorty's—on what the hunters were doing and how they were doing it. If the hunters were not successful, Shorty would at least know what didn't work!

The other hunters knew it was time to call it a night. They also knew they had to keep an eye on that weird Andrew guy. There was something bubbling underneath his angry exterior. But now, it was time for Friday night shuteye on this standalone mount.

Three professional Bigfoot hunters, three mountain men, three female professors, plus one spy; all ten of the hunters would spend the next three days using their talents, their ingenuity, and their wits to get the job done. Who would win the million dollar reward? And in the end, what would it cost them? Who would discover that their ideas were the best? On the other hand, who would feel deceived and defeated? But most importantly, would Shorty end up being the true King of the Mountain with his Bigfoot finally under lock and key? Oh, and one more question: Was Bigfoot watching the ten little hunters right now?

Chapter 3
Three Mountain Men

Being overweight and dumpy in frame, Franklin had kept his head down and his eyes averted throughout his high school years. He rarely smiled and was soft spoken. His mother bought his clothes extra-large for growth, she said. Franklin was always trying to fill the sizes by eating more than he needed. His mother fixed all the foods he enjoyed, even when they weren't especially good for him, feeling guilty that she didn't work harder at preparing nutritious meals a long time ago when Franklin was small. Now, she simply wanted to bring a smile to his face, so she supplied the foods that seemed to make him happy.

Wearing his black hair long, with bangs practically covering his eyes, his dark rimmed glasses shielded him as well. He didn't want anyone to see him, much less pay attention to him. Every day in school was a struggle to stay invisible long enough to get through the day and get back out to the hills he loved.

But all in all, getting through high school was not hard for Franklin. He didn't see any use in some of the high school courses, or what good they would do in his later life. Was there really a use for geometry or social studies or biology? Well, maybe biology. Being out of high school was a relief, but he did miss sneaking a peek at the girl sitting at the desk across from his in the next row. He would watch her sometimes, as she tucked her hair gently behind her right ear, her head cocked to the side while she read the text book, oblivious to him. He admired the curve of her cheek and the long neckline of her blouse that curled around and dropped to the top of her breasts. She managed to thump her pencil in rhythm to his heartbeat. *How did she do that?* There was something intriguing about the synchronicity. Maybe it was fate. Maybe she would one day look deep into his eyes and fall instantly in love with him. But then he would remember what she looked like *and* what he looked like. He immediately dismissed any thought of being with a girl.

Franklin enjoyed his job timbering parcels of land. As time went on, he sweated his way into a slimmer, more manly physique. He stood taller and now his muscles could be seen through his shirt. With strength and stamina, he spent longer hours outdoors, and not so much time indoors, eating. He still wore his hair long though, to hide his face.

Bubba, Franklin and Jimbo grew up together, inseparable since grade school. In the foothills, Bubba's house sat a good distance in the woods from the dirt road. It made for a long morning trek to the bus stop. He always knew his friends, Jimbo and Franklin, would be waiting for him to pop out of the brush, using his own shortcut path to the meet-up place. From there, the three would kick rocks or throw sticks on the way to the bus stop, joking around with each other as they walked and talked about what had happened at school the day before. School was a lifeline to the outside world for the three of them, but school and the world were also intimidating and complicated, with shyness being their common denominator.

It was on the narrow footpath that Bubba first encountered Bigfoot, his only sighting. But it was enough for a lifetime. His two regrets were not having a camera and not having his friends to validate the chance encounter. But he never regretted the sighting, although, at the time, he wet his pants. He had knelt to tie his shoelace and over his left shoulder, he heard a snapping sound of a large limb being cracked in two. Rising to look into the tall brush, he came face to face with a startled Bigfoot. First, a putrid smell slapped him silly. Then, those dark penetrating eyes paralyzed him. Bigfoot was larger than he had ever imagined. A thunderous growl escaped his brown, prickly muzzle. Bubba didn't think or have time to puff up large, making himself intimidating. His body instantly produced a scream, as strong and natural as could be, although shrill. Both shocked to be in the company of the other, his high pitched scream sent Bigfoot back into the timberline.

From that point on, Bubba carried a camera in his backpack and one in his jacket. All three boys worked part time in the forest during high school, felling trees and hauling them to the lumberyard, using a horse to pull the logs in place. Bubba always knew he would be prepared to capture Bigfoot, at least on film. Now, many years later, he was still prepared. After all this time, he hoped he would get another opportunity to see Bigfoot again. He needed to know that he hadn't dreamt the whole thing. With time, his encounter was fading and getting harder to speak as truth.

Bubba, Jimbo and Franklin led very sheltered lives, not mingling often enough with other people, especially girls. Their parents lived sheltered lives as well. For Bubba, it was getting harder and harder to remember very much about his mother since she had died when he was young, and his father stayed so busy, caring for the house and property. Bubba had pretty much raised himself, getting himself to school and then to his timber job. The forest felt like home to him.

Bubba once asked Jimbo and Franklin about their encounters with girls. None of them had any experience with the opposite sex, although Bubba once had a crush on a female classmate. She was blonde with pretty blue sparkly eyes and on Wednesdays, she wore a little cheer-leading outfit that fit snugly to her body, exposing bare legs, long and strong. She never spoke to him and she never once looked his way. It was just as well, he probably would have died from bashfulness.

Walking the forest, working the land, guiding the horse, Bubba took pride in his work. After work, he enjoyed any time he could spend with his buddies. They did tease Bubba every once in a while, sending Bigfoot yelps up into the night air. Bubba knew what he saw and there was no changing that. He told himself that they were just jealous that they hadn't seen Bigfoot. What if all three had seen Bigfoot? Talk about excitement! That would have been the highlight of their lives, coming face to face with Bigfoot. For Bubba, it was an exhilarating, heart-stopping moment.

When he was in high school, and trying to be cool, Jimbo asked to bum a cigarette from one of the football players, who was sitting with his buddies on the top steps of the gym. Being a member of a tough football clique, the football player saw Jimbo as a runt, an outsider, that needed to learn a lesson.

"Sure. You can have a cig!" The player pretended to offer the pack of cigarettes to Jimbo. Jimbo, feeling cool and now a part of "the team" reached for the pack. "But how about a can instead?" In one smooth move, the player was up. Immediately, he grabbed Jimbo by the shirt collar, spun him upside down and stuffed him into the nearest garbage can.

As the laughing players left the scene, coming to his aid were Bubba and Franklin, two people he could forever depend upon. They rescued Jimbo from the trash, with his legs sticking up out of the can and thrashing wildly, trying to tip over the can with no luck.

No attempt was made to repeat the performance. Jimbo knew his place now. He knew who his friends were and would remain loyal to them. He was happy to be a part of their lives, to walk almost shoulder to shoulder, if he stood on his tippy toes, and to know there was someone there who had his back.

Small in stature, he was generally unnoticed by any of the female classmates and he had no interest in sports or after-school club activities. He liked hanging out with his two friends and he liked being in the woods, where nothing was expected of him. He loved the tranquility of the forest and the stillness of the earth.

Now, all three were in on a once-in-a-lifetime opportunity to hunt and capture Bigfoot, something none of them could pass up. No one knew the woods better than they, and no doubt, they were going home with that reward.

CHAPTER 4
ONE RV AND THREE WOMEN

Through dark rimmed glasses, Franklin watched the tall, stylish woman leave the bonfire with her two friends. All three women had food stuffed in their pockets, dropping some as they walked. *How strange*, he thought. *Who the hell are they?* He knew the women would be okay in the parking lot, wearing those sandals, but they would be in big trouble in the wilderness with that footwear. He watched as they climbed aboard the old, used camper, lighting it within as they moved deeper inside. He gathered the fallen packets of hot chocolate and retreated into the dark night.

Rhonda's mother had been more of a child than she ever was. So Rhonda had to take on responsibilities a lot sooner than most girls her age. When her father left her mother, Rhonda, at age eleven, stepped up and tried to be brave, since her mother didn't seem to care what happened to them. She knew her mother was heartbroken; so was she. But someone had to hold things together. Then and there, Rhonda put herself in charge. She held her mother's hand through thick and thin. She was holding her mother's hand when she took her last breath. Always dependable, always tough, always the strong one.

Rhonda slipped off the long metallic vest and then the sandals. "Shut up you two!" Rhonda bellowed at Denise and Lulu, who were arguing over who was going to get the upper bunk. There was a bunk above the driver's seat, with a pop-up section that extended the roof and allowed air to circulate through the screens on two sides. It was a secluded nest, opposite the crowded rear compartment, with its shower and bathroom.

Rhonda emptied her pockets to pull out a coin and flipped it in the air. "Call it!"

Lulu yelled, "Heads!"

The coin came down in the palm of Rhonda's hand and with fluid grace, she immediately flipped the coin onto her left arm, just above her beautiful gold watch and sparkling diamond tennis bracelet.

"Heads! Lulu, you get the front bunk." There, settled.

Denise stomped to the rear of the camper with her belongings and crammed everything in the tiny cabinets, knowing there wasn't enough room for all that she brought. She hated to listen to Rhonda bark out orders. She hated that Lulu always seemed to get her way, no matter what.

Rhonda pulled in the last of their gear as the security guards finished loading, in the cargo-hold, the food supplies, water, all the traps, carts and whatever else the hunters needed for their three days in the woods. Rhonda was to drive the camper up the mountain, bringing along all that the hunters would need to set their traps. Hopefully they would bring the hunt to a successful end. She was relieved knowing they were housed on this trip. Although this was not luxury comfort, no way was she looking forward to camping, with sleeping bags and tents, up the mountain, in no telling what kind of weather. But the most important thing about this trip was proving there is no Bigfoot. And proving to all those idiot men that there was no such thing EVER. Hunting Bigfoot was just another one of their fantasies—any reason to not live in the real world, as she saw it.

"Hunting Bigfoot was another reason for men to go off and leave their family behind. To abandon their responsibilities, to forget their duty to wife and child, to roam free without a care in the world, to never look back at the destruction in their wake!" Rhonda emptied her shirt pockets, skirt pockets, and purse of the stolen food. The anger toward her dad ran deep.

Denise and Lulu had heard this rant many times before.

The cynical Rhonda was now slamming her belongings around in the tiny cubbyhole of a room. *Come hell or high water*, she was going to prove, once and for all, that Bigfoot is merely a figment of men's tiny brains.

"Get some rest, girls! Tomorrow, we will make plans on how to NOT catch Bigfoot! We are simply here to do research and in the end, we will show A) that there is no Bigfoot, and B) that men are losers with a capital L. We can write reports on the topic of "Bigfoot Fantasy" and show the world that men are nothing but imbeciles! Hunting Bigfoot. What a joke!" With vigor, she snapped the sheet flat, out across the bed and slapped the sheet around the corners of the worn out mattress. She then climbed onto the narrow bed and tossed and turned, unable to find a comfortable spot.

Small for her size, Lulu was cute and quite frankly, never taken seriously. She was the smartest girl in high school and then in college. While having no common sense, she was the youngest member of Mensa at the age of twelve. As a biologist with a PhD in Genetics, she came along on this journey in hopes of discovering some new species, their environment, and maybe new adaptations of underlying organisms. She hoped that there was a Bigfoot but would never ever utter that in the presence of Rhonda ("the Rototiller," Lulu's secret name for Rhonda, since she tore up and plowed under anything in her way). She hoped that Bigfoot would give up some of its secrets of family dynamics, survival in severe weather, disease or the lack thereof, scarcity of food and its effect on the life expectancy. She hoped this mountain held a goldmine of information on the incredible existence of Bigfoot. Then this whole trip would be worthwhile. She just had to keep her expectations and hopes to herself. She dreamed she would discover the underpinnings of the great mystery called Sasquatch. She would help the world by divulging Bigfoot's secrets of successfully evading mankind.

With that thought, Lulu got ready for bed.

Denise was the prissiest of the three professors. She liked luxury. She liked fine dining. She liked cleanliness. She hated the camper with its smell of dirty socks and damp mildew. The smell was stronger in the rear of the camper, near the bathroom and shower. She didn't see how she was going to get any sleep, how she was going to survive on camper food or get free of unseen organisms living on every surface. She tiptoed, hoping not to pick up any living bacteria from the grungy floor, although she had on socks and slippers. She had thought to bring extra sheets and pillowcases, thank goodness. But would that be enough of a barrier to creepy, crawling things? Her idea of roughing it was eating at a diner or sleeping at a motel. She saw herself as a princess, even at her age. She had given up hope of finding a prince but never gave up the feeling of being treated royally. Her dad made sure she was well taken care of and wouldn't have to worry, with or without a man. Funny that she was a professor of social anthropology, the study of relationships among persons and groups. She couldn't hold a relationship together if her narrow, selfish life depended on it.

"By the way, we need to call someone to come fumigate this camper. It stinks to high heaven back there." She pointed to the rear of the camper, wishing she could have an instant do-over of the coin toss. Maybe she would pay closer attention and get the call in ahead of Lulu.

From the back of the camper came a reply. "Listen, Princess, we have a job to do, so buck up here! Besides, there is no one to call out here on this mountain!" Denise realized that her problem was of no interest to Rhonda or Lulu and that it was time to get serious about this project at hand. The sooner this thing was over, the sooner she could take a bubble bath to soak off all the "cling-ons" from the smelly old camper.

"Well, we have to look like we're interested in finding Bigfoot. We have to pretend that we're after the reward. Otherwise, these imbeciles will throw us out of the hunt." Denise continued, "So I suggest we use ropes to snare the imaginary Bigfoot, like I saw in the old movies. When they heard a commotion, it was someone or something caught upside down, hanging by the ankle from a rope attached to a large tree." Rhonda had come to join the other two women at the little fold-away table. She stopped filing her nails and tapped the emery board against her lips, thinking.

Lulu chimed up. "It wouldn't be hard to accomplish and it would be easy to disguise the rope so Bigfoot won't even know what hit him!" As soon as the words came out of her mouth, Lulu instantly ducked.

"Who's the imbecile?" Rhonda pounced. "How many times have I told you they DON'T EXIST!" Lulu would have to be careful with her words. She knew they probably didn't exist but she could secretly hope.

"We have to participate in the hunt, Rhonda. What do you suggest we do?" Now Denise was getting impatient with Rhonda. "We came on this… this… excursion at your prompting. What do you have in mind?"

"We will put one foot in front of the other." Rhonda muttered, with an idea of how to "act" like they were hunters. Suddenly she brightened. "Yes! Let's put our best foot forward." And she giggled to herself. Denise and Lulu looked confused but knew from past experience that Rhonda was up to something. Rhonda was brilliant. She had a keen sense of research skills, so other professors looked to her for guidance, especially Lulu and Denise. This trip should prove to be useful to them and their careers. Any new research for their university would help with the success of all involved.

CHAPTER 5
ONLY THE FIRST NIGHT

She snuggled under the light blanket, finding a comfortable spot right away. Lulu had never seen anything like it. The pop-up feature above the bed was sheer genius. There was fresh air and she didn't have to breath the stinky, enclosed air of the damp smelling camper. It smelled like a mix of pervasive mold spores and old Pine-sol. She hated that the foul aroma had caused her nose to twitch, like it does just before a sneeze. She inhaled a large breath. Yes, she lucked out with the pop-up canopy above the bed and the fresh air it provided. Although one had to be a bit of an acrobat to get to it, the cubbyhole bed over the driver's seat was just the right size for her. Perfect.

Lulu smiled, remembering it was she who had thought of capturing Bigfoot with the ankle noose. That involved very little supplies and it also showed that they were serious about capturing the elusive mountain monster. What if they did capture Bigfoot? "Oh my God, Rhonda will have a heart attack." With that thought, Lulu didn't know whether to smile or feel ashamed. Yawning, she remembered Rhonda's words: "Bigfoot or Big Fantasy." She was covertly hoping there was something out there to catch. Bigfoot, the ultimate survivalist. "Wow, what it could teach the world!" As a biologist, she would jump at the chance to study the living habits of the ever-evasive yeti. But for now, she was tired.

The singing crickets lulled Lulu to sleep. She drifted, enjoying the dream of lying in a hammock and the great outdoors. She smiled as the clouds drifted and formed countless creatures. Her smile broadened when birds flew into and out of frame of the ever-changing sky-scape. With a loud, shrill call, she spotted a large redheaded woodpecker in the tree way above her head. It pecked and dug and hopped and pecked some more. The air was clean and fresh and vibrant with dynamic movement, much like a Van Gogh painting. Not too far away, she could hear water splashing, bubbling and rippling in the moonlight. She drifted into a forest of perfection, into the still, calm place deep within her that was dark, comforting and silent like a vaulted fortress.

Denise didn't sleep a wink. She fought the covers all night, first hot and then cold, flinging the blanket on and then flipping it off again. The mattress, if one could call it that, was chunky and unforgiving, and especially rough on her face. She awoke, startled that her face was on the roughly textured, pilling cover of the mattress, and not on the sheet she had meticulously covered the nasty thing with. "What the heck!" She jumped up, away from the bed, angry that the sheets had come completely off the lump of a mattress. Her hands went to her face where the roughness of the filthy mattress still lingered. "BLOODY HELL!"

While remaking the bed, Denise scratched several spots on her legs, thinking mosquito bites were to blame. "Can this get any worse? I hate this crap," she mumbled as she crawled back between the sheets and fought to find a lump to settle on, to drift back to a peaceful moment of rest, to forget where she was and dream of being home, safe in her bed. Try as she might, the itchy spots on her legs seemed to have jumped to her arms. Her brain was playing tricks on her now, making her believe there were bug bites on her back and around her waist. Exhausted, she finally slept.

There was a knock at the door. Denise wrapped the robe around her as she made her way to the door of the camper, wondering who would be knocking in the middle of the night. Expecting to find a peep hole, she was surprised at the small, diamond-shape window in the door above her head, and she stood on tiptoes to see out into the moonless night. She cracked the door open and just then, the face of Bigfoot moved into the light spilling from the room. Before she could slam the door shut, a big, hairy foot filled the open doorway. It was humongous! Denise went running, screaming and tripping over logs and sticks, until finally, she fell into the burning embers of the bonfire.

Denise drew in a sharp breath as she sat straight up in bed. It was morning. The camper's moldy smell greeted her and she recalled where she was and that Bigfoot had been a dream. But her face and arms felt like they were on fire. She pulled herself out of bed and traipsed to the front of the drab camper where Rhonda was pounding on the faucet, trying to get water to come through the pipes. Denise saw Lulu sitting at the tiny table, waiting for someone to make breakfast. Lulu had been awakened by Rhonda's cursing the kitchen sink. Lulu sucked in a big breath of surprise as she looked at Denise, who was covered with red, angry spots. Denise's face looked like she had a very bad case of raging, teenage acne, ten times over.

Lulu couldn't speak. Wincing at the sight, Lulu could only point with one hand at Denise's face, while covering her wide open mouth with the other, which sent Denise running to the bathroom mirror.

The screams were real this time. Denise ran back to Rhonda and pleaded for help. "What do I do? WHAT DO I DO?" she begged, her hands flailing about her face. Rhonda couldn't hide her disgust at the sight but tried to get control of the situation. "Let's just take a minute and try to figure out what is going on." Rhonda and Lulu practically tripped over each other as they ran to the mirror to see if they were afflicted, but Rhonda hogged the mirror, keeping Lulu from it.

Denise was in a panic. Trying to get the water to run in the kitchen sink so she could wash away the spots, she pounded the handles of the faucet with the extremely large wrench Rhonda had been holding earlier.

"What is going on here?" Denise could not get the water to turn on and she was becoming more exasperated with every passing second. Suddenly, itching all over, she ran screaming to the shower stall, thinking warm water would help wash away some of the itch.

"Has anyone tried the shower yet in this thing?" She was scared the water might come out brown, but she frantically started the shower. "What do we have that I can put on these bumps?" Her quivering voice was high and shrill.

Being in the backcountry, there was no cell service or Internet service, so they could only guess as to what was happening to Denise. After some discussion, Lulu thought it might be wise to use clear nail polish on the bumps. "Could the bumps be chigger bites? And who has that much nail polish?" Rhonda quizzed her. "We'd have to dip Denise in a vat of nail polish, looking at all the bumps that are visible."

"Just don't make that comment in front of Denise. We have to remain calm, for her sake. Where do you think she got all those bug bites? Did you feel any mosquito bites last night?" Rhonda was checking her own legs.

Rhonda looked at Lulu. "Well, you don't look so hot yourself, kiddo." Just then Lulu sneezed. And then she sneezed again and again.

Lulu had sneezed like that in the "sky" bed, where she tried to sit up in bed but there was no headroom. Realizing that it was dripping, she wiped her sleeve across her nose. She felt stuffy and her eyes barely opened. She had rolled from the bed and dropped down to the floor at the front windshield. Taking a seat at the table, she forgot about her nose when she saw Rhonda banging on the faucet. She certainly forgot about it when she saw Denise. But now, she ran to the rear-view mirror hanging from the big windshield. She did not recognize who was looking back at her. Her eyes were mere slits, her nose bulbous, hot and red. The night air must've been full of pollen. She decided her problem was a lot worse than Denise's inflamed body.

Just to make sure there were no creepy crawlers on her body, Rhonda slipped into the shower after Denise finished. It was awful what was happening to Denise and poor, little Lulu. The camper was never checked, as far as Rhonda knew, by anyone in authority, not really sure of the protocol when renting a used piece of equipment. This was a first for these ladies and they were totally out of their element. Rhonda felt bad for them, but she couldn't be held responsible for all the problems of the world, now could she?

The shower had a little more force than Rhonda expected. She stepped into the shower and yanked the shower curtain across. Just as she turned to face the stream of warm water, she glanced up to see the humongous wrench heading right for her face, with no time to react. In an instant, the large piece of metal slammed into her cheekbone, just below her left eye. Immediately, the area began to swell, even before the pain set in.

"What the f@&#!" She grabbed her head, trying to figure out what had just happened. When she pulled the curtain across, her hand had hit the edge of the small ledge at the top of the stall, and also caught one end of the wrench, sending it airborne. WHAM! Close to blacking out, she stumbled around, grabbing and twisting, wrapping the curtain around her like a mummy. She went crashing into the closed bathroom door, hitting the door handle just below her right eye.

Curled up on the floor, she momentarily blacked out. Then she shook herself from the darkness.

"What moron leaves a wrench up there?"

She remembered Denise grabbing the wrench in the kitchen, trying to pry some water from the pipes for her red, itchy face. With no luck, Denise had fled with the wrench in hand. Now, Rhonda was going to kill her, as soon as she could get up from the floor. She could feel her face swelling on both sides.

"Well, it is a good thing we are out in the woods; no colleagues to see my face like this." Rhonda finally freed herself from the curtain. "And I need to find a good spot to bury Denise's body!" Rhonda stormed out of the bathroom, ready for bear.

CHAPTER 6
FRANKLIN HELPS OUT

There was a knock at the camper door. The women inside looked at each other, wondering who it could be. They were a sight, with Lulu's big red, runny nose, Denise's hive covered body, and Rhonda's two black eyes. With the other two women feeling self-conscious, Rhonda ventured to the door and cracked it open.

Franklin briefly looked at Rhonda, jammed his hands into his pockets and turned to look away from her. He wasn't sure what was wrong with Rhonda but she didn't look like the same woman from the bonfire.

"I thought I'd let you know that there was a bear in our camp area last night, so be careful how you wander around out here." Franklin didn't know where to look or what to say and he couldn't wait to get away from the RV.

"Oh. Okay. Thank you," Rhonda slammed the door shut.

Now the women weren't sure of what to do. They were not feeling well anyway, so it seemed wise to stay in.

"I think it was the fresh air that did me in." Lulu stated.

"Well, I can't sleep on that bed. Look at me!" Denise wailed.

"Keep it together, girls!" Rhonda exploded. "I don't care what we look like! We have a job to do and we're gonna do it! Do you understand me?" Rhonda looked insane, with her bandit eyes, her bruised cheeks, the veins in her neck throbbing.

Lulu blew her nose while Denise scratched under her arm with one hand and scratched her butt with the other. Rhonda seethed, angry about the black eyes and angry with the two cry-babies she had to coddle and now, a bear was thrown in the mix. *Perfect! Just Perfect!*

Rhonda pulled on her clothes and stepped outside. She was in such a mood that even a bear would run from her. "We have to get this done and get out of here" she quietly vowed to herself. She immediately stopped and looked around.

The air was still and crisp. Birds were singing. When was the last time she had heard birds singing? There was very little noise, but the forest was alive, vibrant. Sitting on a stump, Rhonda felt the sunshine on her arms and raised her face to it. *Ughhhh!* Her eyes ached.

Déjà vu! Lingering in the sunlight, Rhonda—for the first time in a long time—let herself remember sitting in the sunshine with her mother, on a blanket, sharing a picnic. What a wonderful day they had had together. Now, this day was very much like that day. The world was alive, almost crackling with possibilities. The memory was strong and wonderful. Maybe she *could* let go of some of the anger and remember the good times she had with her mom.

Stepping out of the shadows, Franklin made himself known. Squinting, Rhonda looked at him and reluctantly decided to be nice. "Thank you for the warning about the bear." She looked at the ground because she could tell Franklin was uncomfortable looking at her.

Stammering, he asked if everything was okay. Rhonda smiled, picked up a piece of pine straw, and fiddled with it, trying to explain to Franklin what had happened in the camper shower.

"You got a real beaut, that shiner!" Franklin offered. His black bangs falling to the side of his face as he tilted his head.

"Yeah? Which one?" Rhonda teased him.

"Well, your whole face is a shiner." Franklin wasn't sure he should have said that.

"Thanks for that observation." Rhonda felt embarrassed—the first time in a long time, if ever.

"Is there something I can fix in the camper?" Franklin offered again, nervous to be talking to a beautiful woman, even if she did have a purple face. He had noticed her the previous night, stuffing hot chocolate packets in her underwear, and thought she was very pretty. Rhonda looked at him long and hard and then decided he was harmless. She smiled.

"It would be great if you could get the water to work in the kitchen sink. Let me see if the girls are dressed." Rhonda went in the camper and checked to make sure everyone was clothed. Rhonda came back out, followed by Denise and Lulu.

"Holy moly! What have you girls been up to?" Franklin was shocked by the faces of the other women, both with red, aggravated skin. Denise pulled at her shirt and explained her night on the mattress. Lulu sneezed again and again, wiping her bulbous nose with a wet tissue. There were small pieces of tissue hanging from her nose.

"Sure, I can check the water," Franklin nodded, "but could you pull the camper up to the Rainwater Cove marker? Most of us moved up there earlier this morning. My backpack and some supplies are up there."

Rhonda motioned for the ladies to get back in the camper. "We'll

24

be up in a minute." She watched Franklin head up the mountain. As Rhonda jumped into the driver's seat, she tried to remember if she had ever asked a man for help. Nothing came to mind.

A thousand feet up the hill, Franklin pulled the mattress from the RV and propped it up in the sunlight. He was thinking she must have gotten chiggers from the area around the bonfire or there were ants that bit her. He didn't investigate her bites, being too bashful to get that close. He left to go to his camp area to get some antihistamine for both ladies. Soon he was back. He brought a bar of black soap and instructed Denise to get in the shower and to leave the soap on as long as she could stand it. Psychologically, this might help her "wash away" whatever it was that caused the bites because he really didn't know what the true problem was. He told them that the mattress needed to stay out in the sunshine and maybe the night, just to make sure nothing was still on it. Denise would have to sleep sitting up, in the passenger seat. He doled out the antihistamine. Rhonda didn't want to be left out, hoping it would help her sleep.

Franklin proceeded to check the water in the kitchen. He only had to open a valve underneath the sink. He instructed the ladies that they had to go easy on the water, since there was a limited supply on a camper. *Limited water? They had never heard of such.* After checking on each woman, Franklin walked back to his camp, happy that he could be of service. He didn't feel so invisible. Actually, he felt optimistic and positively manly.

CHAPTER 7
WELCOME THE PROFESSIONALS

Saturday morning was brilliantly clear. The Professors were just getting their first day started but the Bigfoot Professional Hunters had been up and at 'em for quite some time. Clarice was out searching for the best place for her pink Princess castle tent. Clive thrived on the mountain air, this being one of his favorite places on earth, and he was out seeking two strong trees for his amazing hammock trap. And Matthew was sizing up tree limbs, big enough to support him and be comfortable because he didn't know how long he would be up a tree waiting for Bigfoot.

The Mountain Men were out searching, too.

Lagging behind them all was Andrew. He was looking for a Bigfoot path along the stream, marking soft spots to dig holes for his Slap Ankle Bracelets. He was working for Shorty, as the cook.

However the others didn't know he was Shorty's spy. Regardless, his intent was to trap the burly beast. Shorty Tubbottom was not going to swindle Andrew out of his chance to collect the reward. And he would make sure the other hunters didn't either!

All of the hunters had pull carts loaded with their daily supplies and traps. The storage compartment on the camper held their stockpiles and they simply pulled what they needed. Except for the RV, they were all on foot, moving steadily up the mountain. The hunters were not together. They fanned out, so as to not allow others to see their traps or their hunting style. Friday night's dinner had been the opportunity for them all to meet, but then they were left up to their own devices. The consensus among all the hunters was to move up the mountain, stalking Bigfoot, until there was no place else to go. Certainly by then, Bigfoot would fall into one of their traps.

So here it was Saturday morning, all shiny and bright, with a comfortable temperature of sixty degrees. Shorty Tubbottom's mountain was now the hunter's domain and they were all ready to get down to business. Scouting out the perfect spot was the first action of each morning. They left the pavilion behind, along with the first three trail markers and landed at Rainwater Cove. If they caught nothing the night before, they would move on

26

up the mountain and begin again, finding the right spot to set up the traps. They would congregate in the early afternoon to "chew the fat" and rest while they waited for evening to descend, to begin the Squatch Watch.

Andrew brought clackers with him. In camp, he would pull out the clackers and make noise, hoping to attract Bigfoot. The clackers would also become a signal to gather. The other hunters would follow the sound of the clackers and they would meet up on common ground at the campsite. The clackers were what children would spend hours using to aggravate their parents, with its loud, obnoxious popping, smacking together, over and over and over.

Just beyond the tall, swaying grass, Clarice found a nice, cozy clearing in a thicket of large bushes and a couple of old oak trees. It had very little underbrush and was quite level. This would make a good spot for the Princess castle tent that she had carted up the hill in a wagon. The castle tent would certainly entice a young, female Bigfoot into her camp. She had twinkling, battery-operated lights to hang inside it and a blanket with nice, plump pillows. A Bigfoot youngster would find this too irresistible to pass up. Once inside, the large, hidden rope net would trap the lounging creature, securing her in the web. *Go for the young. The others will follow.* Much like Rhonda, Clarice, always the skeptic, thought this was the way to go and the only way she would know for sure that Bigfoot really exists. She would no longer have to rely on hearsay, or mystery skat, or the opinions of the "sight-seers" who happened to glimpse a large "something or other." Clarice was a true scientist; positive proof was her only way.

She began laying out the large rope net and then climbed up the tree to secure her rope pulleys.

It took all afternoon to get the basic foundation of the net in place. Plus, she had to hide the ropes with lightweight camouflaged vines she had brought with her in the wagon. Once the net was in place, Clarice erected the castle tent. It was lovely, with pink panels decorated with flowers and unicorns. Inside, she attached the twinkling lights and spread out the blanket, then fluffed the pillows. Strings of bright pink beads were scattered about. She avoided the very center of the tent, for there was the sensor for the rope net. Once weight is put upon the center of the blanket, *whooshh!* Up goes the unsuspecting ape. She spritzed the outer tent with "Midnight Oasis," a perfume she was sure would allure male and female alike.

Clarice backed away from the tent and dropped a few morsels of dry kitty food, the smelliest she could find. She continued to leave the kitty kibble along the trail as she got further away from the tent. She was growing anxious. This could be it. She could really capture a Bigfoot. She smiled to herself. *There has never been any proof that Bigfoot exists.* She hoped to one day see for herself the mighty Bigfoot. In the meantime, she must remain professional. Her team was counting on it.

"Even bears like hammocks!" Clive chuckled as he set up the super large hammock to demonstrate its usefulness for Clarice and Matthew.

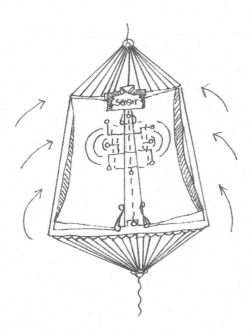

They were not so sure that this was going to be helpful in catching Bigfoot. "It will probably work just as well as your castle bedroom." Clive ventured, poking fun at the unimpressed Clarice.

The hammock had extra hardware on each end and along each long side was an iron rod that supported the edges of the hammock. Those rods were encased in the fabric so they were not noticeable at all. The fabric was an extremely durable parachute material, hard to puncture or cut but was colorful and as bright as the new day.

As soon as Clive finished setting it up, he asked Matthew to pretend to be Bigfoot and see what Bigfoot would think and do with the over-sized hammock. Clarice and Clive backed up and gave Matthew plenty of room to play. Matthew circled the hammock, which was attached to two large tree trunks. He eyed the hammock, moved to the edge and nudged it. The hammock responded in gentle swaying. Matthew pretended to be startled, and jumped back away from the hammock. Clive and Clarice laughed at his silly antics.

This time, Matthew pushed the hammock harder and it glided easily back and forth. Then, Matthew circled the hammock again and decided to try to climb on the hammock. He backed up to the hammock and pulled it underneath his butt and cautiously sat down. It held him while he rocked ever-so-gently, keeping his feet planted on the ground. He felt comfortable. He was ready to lie back on the hammock but kept his feet on the ground, mainly to thrust himself back and forth while prone. It was fun.

He lifted himself up from the hammock and walked around it again, not sure of how this was ever going to catch a Bigfoot. Finally, he said, "It's time to stretch out in this thing and take a nap!" He aimed his head for the attached pillow and flung himself into the middle of the hammock. As soon as all his weight was in the middle, the hammock sides flew up around him, encasing him in the hammock like a burrito. He thrashed about but could not get free.

Clarice and Clive howled with laughter. "How ingenious!" Clarice shrieked. Clive explained, "The iron rods on the long sides cannot be bent. There is a weight-sensitive mechanism on each end, dead center of the hammock, that allows the metal to 'fold,' sealing the creature inside." *Viola!* Clive bowed, with his arms extended to the hammock that held Matthew inside. Clarice and Clive clapped and giggled. She begged to hear more on how Clive had come up with such a device. He was happy to oblige. After some time, they turned back to the hammock, and heard loud snoring coming from within. Clive gave thumbs up to Clarice and remarked, "Let's hope Bigfoot will feel the same."

Their cohort, Matthew, was setting up his own trap. He adjusted the laser to six feet. It would read and measure the height of any person or thing and when registered, it would trigger the net. The net gun had sensors that were motion activated, so it would swing in the direction of action and sound.

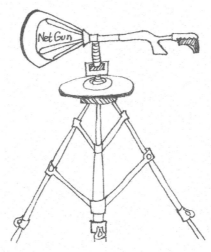

It had taken Matthew months to get accuracy with the net gun. He felt confident that it would tangle Bigfoot up long enough for Matthew to get to him. The only problem was reloading the darn thing. The netting had to be precisely packed, taking hours to meticulously fold, then load into the chamber. Mistakes were costly, time-wise. Now Matthew felt ready. Come evening, he would set up a delicious meal for Bigfoot and let the net gun do its job.

CHAPTER 8
MORE TRICKY TRAPS

Jimbo, Franklin and Bubba thought food was the answer to capturing Bigfoot. Thinking about what satisfies them, as men, would also satisfy Bigfoot. It doesn't have to be fancy, just aromatic. They had each packed a large cooler with frozen, dead animals, which they would leave in strategic spots to lure Bigfoot to his moment of capture. The little dead creatures would be like appetizers, leading Bigfoot from one to another; a meandering buffet, so to speak; until finally, he is caught in the large PullTightBag that he doesn't even know he has entered—until it is too late.

The PullTightBag was a concoction that Bubba dreamt up, thinking of a large fishing net. His was a large macrame bag that closes behind anyone pushing forward into it. Certainly, it has to be big enough to envelope Bigfoot. Bubba used himself to measure and create the gigantic PullTightBag. As Bigfoot wanders into the opening, he smells more food inside. He pushes aside the barriers to the food, shoving deeper into the Bag. As he does so, the opening (like a cable zip-tie) narrows behind him with each step Bigfoot takes, sealing himself in a humongous mesh bag.

Franklin and Jimbo thought it was hilarious when Bubba demonstrated how the Bag worked. Amazingly simple, Franklin and Jimbo thought Bubba to be quite clever. They watched as Bubba, bent in half,

proceeded, sniffing the air for food. Pretending to smell something delicious, Bubba made his way inside the bag, each step causing the opening to
dwindle, getting smaller and smaller until completely closed up. Now came
the real test, in the great outdoors.

Bubba found large bushes, right off the deer trail, that would work
perfectly for his PullTightBag. Hidden on the other side of the bushes, he
constructed a makeshift "room" that enclosed a nice eating area, which he
quaintly called the "bait room." With each step that Bigfoot took inside,
the entranced shriveled, cocooning Bigfoot in the Bag, sealing his fate.
Fragrant smelling food would entice Bigfoot to make his way through the
nicely trimmed opening in the front of the bushes. Bubba used old limbs
and sticks to cover the back side of the chamber and inside vines covered
the ground, hiding the ratcheting line that pulled the entry closed. Limbs
supported the inside area, concealing the huge netted bag, but would give
way, landing on top of Bigfoot. At dusk, he would deliver the delicious,
sleep-aid laced bait.

Bubba's big Bag made Jimbo think of his own trap. He had seen kids crawling through big pipes. He had also seen dogs scramble through pipes as
part of their training routine. His pipe was made of collapsible rings covered with fabric. The pipe has to be an indestructible pipe with no way out,
sealing the Squatch inside as soon as he grabs the food.

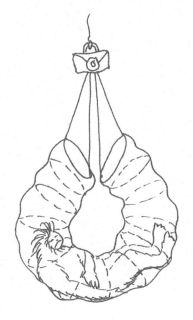

Jimbo thought the big pipe would be enticingly fun for Bigfoot and his companions. He moved up the mountain, at Spotted Bear Point, away from where Franklin and Bubba had been working, and set up the pipe. With metal rings and tear-proof fabric the pipe was brightly decorated, drawing the curious attention of the cryptid. A valued treat would draw him in, keeping him from escaping.

It was tricky, figuring out how the pipe would seal itself off but Jimbo had given it much thought. Using a tree and cables, once the bait was removed from the sensor, the heavy gage wires ringing the outer edges of the tunnel pipe would spring the end openings together. The pipe would tightly enclose the critter inside the doughnut. Jimbo had dreamt of the moment his trap would spring closed, securing his million dollars! And how interesting this would be for a juvenile Bigfoot. To see the food in the middle of the pipe and then to go inside the tunnel, seeking fun and food!

They all worked hard their first morning to get their traps in place. Franklin was thinking along the same line as Bubba. Franklin took the most time in finding the right opening among the trees. He was setting up a zip-line. He searched for a space wide enough so that a body could swing through without getting caught up in limbs. He did have to shimmy up a few times to cut some limbs, but all in all, he managed to construct simple landing platforms on each tree. He finished ratcheting the large cable in place. Bigfoot certainly would enjoy swinging effortlessly from tree to tree in Tarzan-like fashion on the zip-line. All of it was temporary and simply constructed because Franklin would have to take it all down the next morning. Today the trap was near Stand Back Ledge but tomorrow it would be a different place. Each day, the plan was to keep moving up the mountain, squeezing Bigfoot to the top. And hopefully with no place else to go.

As the "chef," Andrew was always on the lookout for animals that would be a quick kill and a quick cook. Since childhood, he had become proficient at using a slingshot. He could track an animal for miles, with it unaware of his presence. However, this trip up the mountain was different. There had been very little rain for the past month and very few footprints, paw prints or hoof prints. With an abundance of dried, crackling underbrush, shadowing a dinner item was near impossible.

Thank goodness, there were coolers packed full of food in the camper. With the dry conditions and his spying duties, he did not have a lot of time to hunt. His contribution to finding Bigfoot was to create delicious aromas that would draw Bigfoot and friends closer to the hunters (and making hunters into prey?)

Andrew stayed a bit behind the groups. He searched the trees for markings. The bucks would scrape the trees with their antlers. He knew that where there were deer, there was Bigfoot. He searched the banks of the slow moving stream along the deer trail at Stoney Creek for soft areas to bury his Slap-Ankle bracelets. He buried five strategic traps along the sloping bank which were connected to hidden chains ringing the nearby trees.

When Bigfoot is trapped, he was instructed, as were all hunters by Shorty Tubbottom, to contact the nearby Rangers to "dart" the creature. However, Andrew was the only one with a radio.

Andrew was sure he had the magic idea, the magic invention, the magic trap of all traps! The Slap-Ankle traps would work just like the wrist slap bracelets, except the ankle traps were metal cuffs that would spring closed when stepped on, snapping two metal bracelets, from opposite sides, around the ankle of Sasquatch. *GOTCHA NOW,SQUATCHIE!* Andrew was patting himself on the back! Little did he know that Rhonda was snooping close by, spying to see what he was up to.

CHAPTER 9
SQUEALS OF DELIGHT

Lulu, the biologist, was interested in the physical characteristics and vital life mechanisms of Bigfoot. While wandering the woods, she hoped to gain insight into the daily life of the mysterious creature. Lulu sought to discover the true essence of the brute, to unravel the riddle of this elusive anomaly. Yet, the woods offered little as far as Lulu could tell. She was beginning to agree with the men, thinking the only way to find out these things was with the capture of the Squatch, but she dared not suggest that within earshot of Rhonda. After all, they were here to further Rhonda's cause—that there is no such thing as Bigfoot!

Springing to her feet, she decided she would gather intelligence by speaking with the men in the camp. *Boy, would Rhonda crown her for that—using intelligence and men in the same sentence.* Lulu meandered over to where Jimbo was preparing a small, smelly critter for bait. Trying not to look or smell, Lulu asked Jimbo to tell her how this rank lure was to work for him. He lifted the stinking sacrifice with loving hands and commenced to explain the significance of smell.

"Bigfoot is always hungry and the aroma of food is quite compelling. I imagine he likes fresh meat just like the next guy but stinky food is also interesting. You must remember that Bigfoot has no fire to cook his food, hence rotting food is on the menu. Sometimes, the smellier, the better-to Bigfoot, mind you." Jimbo added. He blushed, realizing that he was speaking to a beautiful woman who seemed to have a cold, her nose blazing red. He smiled at Lulu.

Lulu turned away from the smelly offering, trying not to puke, but Jimbo's smile was enticing and she wanted to get back to that. Plus, she felt his knowledge would be beneficial to *her* cause, to *her* scientific endeavor. She smiled at Jimbo and said, "I'd love to know more but can we do this without the smell?" They planned to meet later. Jimbo chucked the sacrifice back in the cooler and went to get cleaned up. Lulu left the camp, wondering how the other girls were doing.

Denise's hot skin had begun to calm down. She couldn't help but scratch some of the places, under her arms and around her wrist. The antihista-

37

mine helped a lot. It all must have been getting better because she was interested in getting out and socializing. Her face was not as swollen or as scary. Plus, she wanted to thank Bubba for sharing his meds. Never in a million years would she have been prepared for chiggers, bedbugs, or whatever it was that caused such itching.

Anxious to venture out of the moldy camper, Denise headed for the campsite to see what the others were doing. She needed to talk to Rhonda about, at least, setting out a couple ankle nooses to make it look like they were interested in catching Bigfoot. Being an anthropologist, she was interested in the life and times of the massive beast, its social interactions, its day to day activities. But she knew Rhonda would club her if she even heard her thinking out loud about Bigfoot. Just then a hawk called overhead.

Rhonda had already made her way to the camp area. She saw Franklin seated on the ground. He was working on a part of his zip line. She approached him apprehensively.

"You walk like an Indian, or should I say Native American?" He startled her. He spoke, never looking up. "Whatever do you mean?" She asked.

"Well, you approached me like a scout, tracking footprints, being cautious and quiet."

"Well, apparently I didn't do a good job. You knew I was here. I didn't want to disturb you. But since I am here, what 'cha working on?"

"Oh." Franklin cleared his throat. "One of my ratchets is jammed."

"Sounds like a personal problem," Rhonda teased him. And surprised herself. Franklin didn't understand and kept working.

"I just wanted to thank you for your kindness. As you are well aware, we 'girls' are new at this. I'm Rhonda." She introduced herself.

Franklin nodded but didn't look up. He stopped and listened. Some distance away, a hawk was calling. He sat quietly and motioned for Rhonda to sit down.

"Listen. You hear that?"

"Sounds like a sea gull."

Franklin looked to see if she was teasing him again. She wasn't.

"No. It's a hawk. He's hunting. If he calls, he is hoping to make a scared little critter run. Then he'll swoop down to catch the terrified prey."

"Just like a sea gull, except he's after your French fries."

"Okay." Franklin had never been to the beach.

She studied his face and his hands as he worked. Something about him attracted her. To her, he was good looking. But how could you tell, with all that dark hair and glasses?

"Hey, you brought me luck! It's fixed!" Franklin jumped to his feet and boldly smiled at Rhonda. She was momentarily transfixed. His smile was dazzling. She hadn't expected that.

"Wanna go see the zip line?"

Sure she did. Spying was her new game. Poor Franklin wouldn't know what she was up to. Leaving camp, they walked together up the hill.

"So you're a teacher?"

"A PROFESSOR." She harshly corrected him.

"You sure sound like a teacher." "

A college professor." She softened.

"Have you ever ridden a zip line?"

"No. Is it hard to do?"

"Not at all, I mean, if Bigfoot can do it…" Franklin's voice trailed off, not meaning to insult the PROFESSOR.

Just then Lulu and Denise caught up with Franklin and Rhonda.

"Hey, you two! What's up?" Franklin thought their faces looked better.

"Do you remember Denise and Lulu from the camper? Franklin? Is that right?" Rhonda decided they had better introduce themselves. Franklin nodded.

"Franklin is going to zip me!"

"Oh my!" Denise chided, surprised that Rhonda would even stand near a man. "Ya'll are that close already?"

Again, Franklin did not get the joke.

Franklin motioned for Rhonda to follow him, as he climbed up the wooden slats that he had attached earlier to the tree. On the small platform and from behind, he reached around Rhonda and helped her get into the sling. He instructed her to hang on tight, to enjoy the ride, and cautioned her that the zip-line would escalate high at the end of the line, slowing her to a stop before getting to the platform. He would have to be careful with his calculations about the rise of the line. For someone heavier, the ride would increase in speed. But for Rhonda, he wouldn't have to worry about the zip line at this point. He was becoming skeptical that Rhonda would get any enjoyment out of the ride. She had stiffened abruptly when he reached to help her into the sling. Immediately, her aura had turned to pure ice as far as he could tell.

Franklin told Lulu to run to the other end of the zip line, to climb the slats and to wait for Rhonda to zip to the platform. That way, she could stop Rhonda, if need be, and would have her friend to help her out of the sling. Franklin no longer felt comfortable being near Rhonda.

Franklin set Rhonda in motion, away from him, breezing down the zip line. With a thrilling sense of freedom, she squealed with delight. Never before had she been among the trees, swinging like a carefree child. Magically, she had a new perspective, higher and more enjoyable than she had ever known before. What a blast! Finding the zip line to be exhilarating, Rhonda shouted to her friends, "This is so much fun! I could do this all day!" As she approached Lulu, she beamed from ear to ear.

"Yeah, well, you better start acting like you're here to catch Bigfoot." Lulu whispered to Rhonda, as Lulu stood on the platform behind her.

"Who cares about Bigfoot?" Rhonda was in her own world, finally beginning to enjoy herself.

Lulu thought Rhonda was loosening up some, not so rigid and cold. Maybe it was because they were away from the university life—the stuffy, still life of academia. She thought Rhonda to be quite attractive, well, minus the two black eyes she was presently sporting–and could easily catch a man. But Rhonda might as well be after Bigfoot. No man could soothe Rhonda's aching heart, for it was broken in too many pieces since her dad left.

"Wheeee! Wheeee!" Everyone could hear Rhonda, with a new air of vitality, zipping down the mountain side, over and over again. Franklin watched from afar, not understanding the curt coldness of Rhonda when he was helping her. Rhonda didn't understand her feelings either.

CHAPTER 10
MAYHEM IN THE DARKNESS

Clickety-clack. Clickety clack. Clickety clack. Andrew did a little jig as he used the clackers.

It was time to return to camp for a few hours rest before it got dark. It could be a very busy night for everyone. They were all anxious with anticipation. Not only about catching Bigfoot, but imagine receiving a million dollars—a life-changing amount of money!

The professors wandered into camp, where everyone had finally gathered. The men were surprised to see the swollen face of Lulu, the red hives covering Denise, and the dark raccoon eyes on Rhonda's face. The women smiled and told them it wasn't as bad as it looked, but the hunters weren't buying it. *These women will kill themselves before they make it back down the mountain.*

"Hey Bandit! What happened? Y'all get tangled up with some varmint last night?" (Andrew was not a subtle man.) While the other hunters laughed, Franklin jumped up and defended Rhonda and the girls, stating things were not good in the camper. It needed work before they could get properly settled in. Franklin told Rhonda that he would be over to help get the mattress back in the rickety RV before they moved on. Rhonda thanked him. She, Lulu and Denise were grateful for his kindness since they were really unprepared to be out in the wilderness, as evidenced by their faces.

Everyone settled down for a bite to eat and a quiet rest. Rhonda gathered the professors and suggested that they might, once darkness fell, go and spy on what the others had concocted, to check and see what the "idiot men" had devised. It was research, after all. Rhonda wanted to prove to the other professors, as well as academia, that there was no such thing as a Bigfoot. "This is where the fun begins. This is where I will prove that men are inferior!" Lulu and Denise were beginning to worry about Rhonda's supercilious arrogance.

A hoot owl woke the hunters from their brief nap. It was dark. The professors had returned to the camper and were preparing to slip out under the cover of darkness. With flashlights in hand, they wandered down to the edge of the stream, trying to discover what Andrew had been up to earlier in the day. Rhonda didn't like his boorish attitude and didn't think much of him.

It seems everyone was out nosing around in the dark. Clarice went to see what Jimbo's Big Pipe was all about, sneaking quietly up the mountain. Unbeknown to either, Clive was right behind her, interested in Bubba's PullTightBag. Andrew made the short hike over to Clarice's Castle Tent and peeked inside. All he saw was a messy bed. He couldn't imagine Bigfoot being remotely interested in a fancy-shmancy tent with little glitter lights inside. Close by, he heard a limb crack. Holding his breath, he stood perfectly still. The air and the earth was so dry that even a bunny could be heard. Andrew raised his night vision goggles and looked in the direction of the cracking sound. He scanned the forest, moving slowly and he could see a large heat signature. His heart stopped. *What is that?* He held his breath, waiting for whatever it was to move. It finally took a step and turned to its side. Andrew could tell it was a grazing deer and with that, he let out a big sigh of relief.

Jimbo thought Clive to be on the quiet side. That was reason enough to check out what Clive had in store for Bigfoot. *It's those quiet ones you've got to look out for.* So Jimbo advanced toward the working area that Clive claimed for himself. He moved cautiously, not wanting to alert the others to his movement. Thank goodness the traps were spread out fairly well and no one would know what he was up to. He faded into the dark night.

Soon he came upon the hammock. Jimbo moved carefully around it, searching for lines or hidden traps. He found none. He pushed the hammock and it gently rocked. He felt confident enough to sit on the side of the hammock, where he used his legs to rock back and forth. Suddenly, there was a high pitched scream coming from down the hill. Jimbo jumped to his feet and fled into the night.

In camp, Matthew, Bubba and Franklin were within hearing distance. They grabbed their flashlights and night vision goggles and descended the mountain. Once more, there was another scream. Yep, they had been told that a 'Squatch could sound like a screaming woman. Almost running into each other, they were immediately filled with alarm and anticipation as they tried to determine the source of the screaming.

SHHHHH! SHHHHH! They shushed each other. They stopped in their tracks, listening intently. Coming from the hammock, Jimbo soon joined Matthew, Bubba and Franklin.

As it turned out, Lulu was the one doing the screaming. She was caught in one of Andrew's ankle slap bracelets. Rhonda was trying her best to quiet Lulu before they got caught. She didn't want to heart Andrew scolding them for being in his business. "Just give me a minute to figure out what to do." Rhonda tried to soothe the petrified Lulu.

Up the mountain, Clive was still nosing around, trying to find the bushes where he had seen Bubba working earlier in the day. As he stood up tall, Matthew's net gun released its ropey web, quickly enveloping Clive. Thoroughly startled, Clive started screaming like a twelve year old girl!

Clarice, who was snooping near Jimbo's Big Pipe, thought a screaming Bigfoot was heading her way. She was not certain they truly existed but she wasn't going to find out, now that she was alone in the dark woods. She bolted back to the path and down the hill, picking up speed as she descended, and finally went somersaulting into camp, only to find no one there.

Hearing the scream from up the hill, the men immediately turned around and went racing back up the mountain. DAMN! Two 'Squatches! What are the odds! Maybe there was a whole family and they were trying to befuddle all of them. They listened. They moved up the mountain a little more. SHHHHHH! They stopped and listened again.

 Matthew decided to execute some tree knocking. He used a wooden baseball bat to create a noise similar to what Bigfoot does in the forest when he is signaling others. They listened for a response. There was a crunching close by. In unison, every man instantly raised his night vision goggles to peer into the black night, only to see a family of raccoons making its way down the hill to the stream.

 The forest was eerily quiet.

 Then, Matthew gave a Bigfoot call, loud and long. Again, they listened.

The professors heard that call and became frightened, thinking a Bigfoot was near. Lulu could not contain her frantic squeals, trying to free her foot from the solid, stationery bracelet. It was no use. She hated the woods. She hated the bugs and the forest animals, the fresh air and the isolation. Bigfoot was going to snatch her up and carry her off into the woods, never to be seen again. She hated to think of herself as his *captive in a cave!* Lulu screamed again, trying desperately to free herself. Rhonda and Denise, in their dark hoodies and baggy pajamas, were on their hands and knees, scooping mud away from the slap bracelet.

The men ran down the mountain to where they thought they heard the screaming. Looking through the goggles, they soon spotted three juvenile Bigfoots drinking from the stream, relaxing by the water, or playing tag. They couldn't really tell what they were doing but they looked young and, yep, three *female* Bigfoot creatures were playing near the stream. The vague, heat images were fuzzy, but two were on hands and knees while the other was seated and pawing at them.

The men smiled at each other. *What a sight!* They couldn't believe their luck. This place was swarming with Bigfoot creatures. Maybe each of them would catch a Bigfoot!

"Holy cow! Tonight's the night!" They couldn't contain their excitement.

Rhonda whispered, "If I unbuckle the sandal, can you squeeze your foot out?"

"I don't want to leave my sandal! That's a four hundred dollar sandal!" a frustrated Lulu whispered loudly.

"So I guess Bigfoot won't care if you're wearing shoes!" Rhonda threatened to leave her behind. Lulu allowed Rhonda to unbuckle the ankle strap. Lulu easily slid her slender foot up and away from the bogged down sandal and out of the metal ankle bracelet trap. Another squeal escaped Lulu's lips.

"Shhhh! Come on. We gotta get out of here!" Rhonda ordered her comrades.

"See if you can get my sand…" Rhonda jerked her into the nearby timberline and they scurried up the hill. Lulu grumbled all the way back to the camper, hobbling on one bare foot, hopping and complaining about rocks and sticks that poked her poor pampered foot.

"Shhhhh!" Rhonda stopped in her tracks, throwing her arm up and out to quietly stop the other two professors from proceeding. Rhonda could hear someone up ahead. Flashlights were beaming in the dark.

"Is it Bigfoot?" Lulu squeezed Denise's hand.

"Yeah," Rhonda sarcastically answered Lulu. "He's heard there is a four hundred dollar sandal lost in the woods. Do you think Bigfoot owns a flashlight?!?"

"Oh, shut up, Rhonda!" Lulu had had enough.

The beams of light were coming closer. The professors huddled together. Then, the lights were on them.

"What are you girls up to?" Andrew eyed them suspiciously, even though it was suspicious that *he* was coming from the Castle Tent area.

"Not much. We were watching a raccoon family." Rhonda was trying to cover their tracks while Lulu hid her shoe-less foot. It was curious that Andrew had a flashlight in each hand.

"Why two lights?" Rhonda quizzed him.

"So Bigfoot will think I am more than one person." Andrew grinned, feeling like a genius. Rhonda wanted to club him with one of the large flashlights.

"You always have to be out-thinking Bigfoot." Andrew looked down on the ladies with disdain. "You have to stay one step ahead of him." Andrew sauntered down the hill, leaving the women in the dark. Rhonda was glad she distracted him from asking more questions. "Yeah, how does an idiot out-think a figment of his imagination? Dimwit." She shook her head.

CHAPTER 11
A CAMP FULL OF DISAPPOINTMENT

Sunday morning arrived with no Bigfoot capture on Saturday night. However, they were all about to find that there had been mischief afoot in the wee hours. Up with the sun, Andrew was preparing breakfast. One by one, they began to show up and they found Andrew in a crabby mood.

"Didn't sleep last night?" Clive quizzed Andrew, knowing he probably woke the dead with his screaming like a girl when caught in the net gun's spidery web.

"Yeah, I slept okay. I am just angry because someone took my clickety-clack clackers. They were here on top of my locked supply box. I guess a raccoon was prowling around. But would he take my clackers?"

"Awwww, don't worry, it'll show up. I am sure it's around here somewhere."

Just then, Clarice walked up, frowning and down in the dumps just like Andrew.

"What's up, Buttercup?" Clive smiled at Clarice, trying to cheer her up. He was kind of sweet on her.

"I went to check on the castle tent. And it was messy but it was still standing. The only thing is that one of the pillows is missing. I looked all around but couldn't find it anywhere nearby."

Matthew came storming into camp.

"My net gun discharged last night and it must've caught something but the net was all in shreds! How can that be?" Matthew was mad yet astonished.

Clive quickly changed the subject by stating that his hammock had not been disturbed and that he had already begun to disassemble it, getting ready to move it up the mountain. He grabbed a quick snack and headed back out to load his cart.

The Bigfoot Hunters also decided it was best to gather their traps and head to a new location, to a luckier spot.

Andrew held up a dainty, metallic sandal. This was what he was really mad about.

"Looks like someone was doing surveillance on my traps last night!"

Knowing it belonged to one of the professors, Franklin sarcastically stated, "Ask one of those Mountain Men. It looks like something they would wear!" Jimbo and Bubba laughed at Franklin's joke.

"Okay," said Andrew, "I see how this is. Well, I can't blame you. Those snooty chicks are a whole hell of lot cuter than me! But you don't want to get on my bad side! I would be a bigger help to ya than those 'ladiiiess' if Bigfoot is after ya! Just remember that!"

Andrew threw the skillet and spatula on top of the supply box and left to go back to the creek, to relocate his ankle traps. He shoved the sandal into his back pocket, determined to find its match.

Bubba sat in the morning sun, breathing in the clean air. His PullTightBag didn't even catch a possum. He was disappointed but knew he had another chance to claim that reward tonight. He heard Franklin coming up the dirt road with his empty cart.

"Franklin, I'll be there to help you in a minute to take down the zip line. I just gotta grab my PullTightBag and I'll be along with you."

Franklin was happy for his help. The zip line was time-consuming to set up, with slats being nailed to trees as ladders. And the trap at the end was a real doozy. It had to be precise. Having an extra pair of hands to assist made for safer work.

Jimbo's Big Pipe was still erect. That meant there were no visitors. As disappointed as the others, he began to break it down in preparation for the move up the mountain. The earlier everyone reset their traps, the earlier they could catch an afternoon nap. There'd been very little sleeping last night. As soon as he finished gathering his collapsible pipe, he pulled his cart up the mountain.

Up the hill they all went. They split up to investigate a new location for each of their traps, between the Spotted Bear and the Mountain Laurel markers. Franklin found a great spot for his zip line and it was just before the grocery store. This time, his zip line was a little steeper than he liked, but it would work. Jimbo and Bubba found suitable areas and began setting up their traps.

Soon, Clive arrived to set up his hammock. Andrew pulled his skimpy ankle traps up the mountain, along with Clarice and her special tent. Matthew was still moping, upset about his net gun but super glad that he had brought an extra net to install. He just wasn't sure if it would be wasted again, in the night, by whatever mangled his last net. But then he decided the million dollar reward was worth it and set about measuring and calculating its range.

The professors drove the camper up to Mountain Laurel and parked on the hill side of the road. Andrew pulled his cooking equipment and supplies from the storage cabin under the RV. The professors pretended to set up rope snares for catching Bigfoot. All the guys knew there was no way those women were ever going to catch anything. They were lightly viewed as a non-threat to capturing the reward money.

The Bigfoot Professional Hunters, Clive, Clarice, Andrew and Matthew, didn't mind helping their crew members set up. And the Mountain Men, Bubba, Franklin and Jimbo, did the same for their crew. But truly, this was each man for himself when it came to the reward. Andrew, the cook/camp coordinator was on his own, which suited him just fine. He had plans on catching Bigfoot and claiming the reward for himself. As soon as Bigfoot steps into his slap ankle bracelet trap, he will radio the Rangers. The Rangers were instructed to be on standby. When Bigfoot is caught, by whomever, the Rangers were to go into action. After putting the cryptid to sleep with their dart, they would whisk him away, using a specially made van, with a heavy duty lift harness. Off he would go to his new habitat.

Rhonda walked up to where Franklin was setting up his zip line.

"Can I be your test pilot?" She smiled up at Franklin high in a tree where he was ratcheting the line in place.

"Might be dangerous, you know?" He didn't know how to take her.

"Dangerous and FUN! Just what I like!"

Franklin nodded. "We'll see. Come back this afternoon."

Rhonda sashayed to the dirt road, knowing full well that Franklin was watching her. Her heart skipped a beat and she actually relished the rare feeling.

Denise saw Rhonda coming back to the camper and she ran to meet her.

"Those two black eyes look kinda starry! What have you been up to?" Denise chided her.

"Oh, I just wanted to find out if I could do the zip line later today."

"Right. You mean "do" Franklin, dontcha?"

"Stop, Denise. He's not my type. He's an introvert, and too rugged, and uneducated, and..."

"You stop it! You're ga-ga over him!"

Rhonda did daydream about what it would be like to feel those strong, tanned arms around her waist again. She smiled to herself, feeling a little foolish. But dare she let herself feel a little excited? Then she shrugged off the extraneous feelings and got busy bossing the other professors around, not to be distracted from the job at hand. There was much for the women to study, to prove: That there was absolutely no such thing as a Bigfoot. So far though, nothing was going according to Rhonda's plan. All the mishaps were preventing any research.

Rhonda made her way over to see Andrew, to find out where he was setting up camp for the night. He told her about his clackers being missing, about which she was secretly relieved. She appeared so disinterested that Andrew instantly suspected her of stealing his clackers. He knew one of the women had been snooping around his traps, evidenced by the sandal he found. He then told her about Matthew's net being shredded to pieces, and she jumped at the chance to follow up on that lead.

She decided to find Matthew and hear what had happened. Matthew walked with her back down to where the net gun had previously been set up. Rhonda studied the disjointed net and saw clean cut marks on the roping.

"Unless Bigfoot carries a knife, this was carved up by someone. Look at the knife cuts. They are clean, not torn. Besides, the material is too tough to tear. It had to be a knife. Are you just going to leave it here?" she asked Matthew.

"I was thinking as it disintegrates, maybe the birds could use the fibers for their nests or the ground squirrels could use the netting for their burrows. They have dens, you know?"

"And tiny televisions?" Rhonda was such a know-it-all sometimes.

"Why are you so interested?" Matthew inquired.

"Just trying to figure out if we have Bigfoot in our area, that's all."

Most people looking for Bigfoot light up with enthusiasm at the prospect of finding one. Not Rhonda. Her eyes and voice carried no hope, no true interest in what she was doing.

Matthew watched her walk back up the road, not sure of what to make of her. *She is not a believer, he thought to himself. Makes me no never mind. I am gonna win the reward.* He set off, with long, determined strides, back up the road.

CHAPTER 12
MANY DOWNFALLS

By the late afternoon, all the hunters were gathered at the camp. Everyone seemed to be in better spirits, looking forward to the new night and the revived chance to capture the beast. It was thrilling to think that tonight could be the night that totally changed someone's life. Dreaming about the million dollars was what kept the group moving forward.

Franklin asked Rhonda if she was ready to zip. She was on her feet before he could finish his question. Off they went, while Lulu and Denise made mock goo-goo eyes at each other.

"I've never seen Rhonda with the edges knocked off. She is actually giddy at times. She's acting very girly. So unlike herself. She's even nice once in a while." Denise commented.

"Well, I wouldn't go that far. Maybe less crabby." Lulu lamented.

Franklin instructed Rhonda to climb up the tree after him. Once on the platform, he gave her some heavy gloves and told her how to brake once she started getting close to the platform on the distant tree at the end of the zip line. This was different from the first time she zipped but Rhonda wasn't paying attention, her mind elsewhere. She adored how caring he was, how strong he was. She wished that he could zip with her. He shoved Rhonda off the platform and away she went.

It was exhilarating. Rhonda's delight could be heard throughout the forest. For the first time in a long time, she was laughing heartily. Oh, how incredible, such freedom, she thought to herself as she went streaking through the air. She peered back at Franklin and he was hysterically pointing to the distance, his arms gesturing wildly. When Rhonda looked ahead, the tree was right there, with no time to brake. Rhonda slammed into the platform, knees first, then body, then head. The lights went out.

Denise had seen Bubba taking pictures. She wondered if he had captured anything worthwhile. Bubba loved everything about the forest, about nature. If he could only capture its peacefulness, its quiet reverence, then he would feel satisfied. His camera had been his companion since childhood, when he missed that one opportunity to photograph Bigfoot. He would make sure that never happened again. The camera was part of his outfit now. He had also been known to accessorize his boxer shorts with a camera stuffed in a crudely attached pocket. It was that important to him.

Denise was captivated at his intent. He had not moved a muscle, silently waiting and watching through the lens. His attention was held across the valley, on the ridge, just above the tree line. She tapped him on the shoulder. And with that, Bubba swung mightily around, catapulting Denise away from him and down the hill. Denise went flying, then thumping to the ground, and eventually rolling in the dry underbrush. Bubba was momentarily transfixed, not realizing anyone was within shooting distance, but then immediately went to her rescue. Denise had scrapes about her arms and head but was able to get up with Bubba's help. He picked the dried grass from her hair while apologizing profusely.

Lulu headed back to the camp to find Jimbo. He was preparing another small, dead animal, filling it with strong tranquilizer capsules, enough for a four hundred pound Bigfoot to sleep for quite a while. She waved at him and asked if she could accompany him to the Pipe trap he had set up earlier in the day. He welcomed her to join him, stating that he was going by the small grocery store first to pick up ice for the cooler. He needed to store the dead animals for another day and needed ice to keep them fresh.

"Oh, I might find something I need." Lulu told him.

"Well, don't expect much." Jimbo said. "It has the bare essentials at this time."

"Like what?"

"Ice. Canned goods. Band-aids. Aspirin. Bottled water. That's about it. When Bigfoot is caught and the park opens, then the little grocery store will carry more stuff for the park visitors to buy. You know: Bigfoot hats, Bigfoot tee shirts, Sasquatch soda." He smiled at Lulu.

"What's your name, by the way?" Lulu asked him.

Jimbo cleared his throat and leaned in closer to Lulu and spoke in a deep James Bond voice, "James" he said.

She had heard the others call him Jimbo but she realized now that he was trying to be sophisticated. His brilliant smile caught her off guard. He seemed a little nervous with her presence which she found endearing.

They headed to the grocery store. They bought ice, and for Lulu, a pack of gum, and a roll of toilet tissue. A girl has to shop even when there is nothing to buy. Jimbo returned to camp with the ice and packed the remaining dead critters away in their frozen bed. He and Lulu climbed the dirt road to his Big Pipe. The road was gravelly and uneven and Lulu could see how a sprained ankle could happen, especially in sleek little sandals such as hers. Her feet were dusty and dry, causing the sandals to slip here and there.

"James, what do you do when you're not hunting Bigfoot?"

"Everyone calls me Jimbo. You're welcome to call me Jimbo or," and he cleared his throat and lowered his chin and voice to say, "James."

"Jimbo sounds kind of juvenile, don't you think?"

Jimbo, holding the dead animal in his palms, turned to speak to Lulu just as Lulu slipped. She grabbed Jimbo's arm for support, only to have the dead animal slung onto her chest. Lulu screamed and tried turning away from the dead animal, but went face first down the hillside. Jimbo went scrambling down the hill after her. He helped her get up. Her face was full of gravel and blood, her hair full of broken, dried leaves. She rested her head in her hands while Jimbo tried to wipe away the tiny rocks embedded in her face with the toilet tissue.

Back to the store they went to get gauze and band-aids.

Andrew had sprawled out in a camp chair, with one leg draped over one of the arms.

"Well, lookie here." He couldn't believe his eyes. All three of the professors were bandaged, their heads looking like mummies. Rhonda was almost entirely bandaged, even her eyes looked dead. She ached from head to toe.

"Shut up, Andrew!" She wanted to hurt him. She tried to swing at Andrew but Franklin caught her before she fell down again. Andrew smirked.

"These chicks don't look too good." He smiled at their predicament. "Well, we don't have to worry about them catching the Monster. They can't even catch a break from themselves." Andrew cackled as he rambled around camp.

Actually, no one in camp seemed to care for Andrew. His ego appeared ten times larger than Bigfoot. They all hoped they would not see him win the million dollar reward. That would just be too devastating. They were going to have to double down on getting their traps in optimal shape. Leaving the professors in camp with Andrew, the men headed out to check on their traps and take care of last minute details.

Lulu and Denise, both aching from their falls, tried to do whatever Rhonda demanded, just to get her back to the camper. They managed to get her on one of the carts and transported her. She grumbled and yelped with every bump in the road, and there were plenty. Deeply ridged, the road was dry and uneven. Once inside the rusty, dusty, musty RV, they all collapsed.

Franklin came by to drop off a sedative for Rhonda. The over-the-counter sleep tabs came 100 to a bottle, so he had plenty, for stuffing little dead hors d'oeuvres for Sasquatch. And others who may need them. He thought she would be needing some to get through the night. He instructed Lulu to give it to her as a last resort but Lulu felt it was the last resort already. She doped Rhonda as fast as she could. Then Lulu removed her bandages, hoping the air would heal her face faster. She and Denise took Advil and tried to settle down for a rest, praying that Rhonda's sedative would last until morning. They would all feel better then.

There was a loud banging on the door. Lulu went to see what the problem was. Andrew crammed the sandal in Lulu's face and demanded to know what she was doing, snooping around his traps.

Lulu was flustered but denied it was her sandal.

Andrew threatened her, telling her he had better not find any more evidence of their snooping around his traps. "There will be hell to pay, sweetheart." He spat as he finished the word with a hard T. Lulu winced as the spittle sprayed her freshly un-bandaged face.

"I'll give you back the sandal when you return my clackers, whichever one of you stole them!" He leered at Lulu and Denise.

"Get away from her!" Denise demanded, holding the big wrench over her head, ready to swing at Andrew.

Andrew growled loudly. Together, the women slammed the door in his face. Denise helped Lulu back to bed. Lulu wished she hadn't removed her bandages. She tried not to cry, knowing the salty tears would sting the gravelly pockmarks. She looked like someone had used an ice pick on her face. She wished that Rhonda didn't treat her like a peon. Rhonda certainly didn't view Lulu as an equal. Of course, she didn't view anyone as an equal. What was the use of coming on this trip? To be a spy for Rhonda? What would she gain from all this that Rhonda was putting her through? Her PhD was worth so much more than this low-level surveillance. Closing her eyes, she tried to rest, praying she would keep her face from touching the bed linens or mattress and it would be much better with the morning light.

CHAPTER 13
BAGGED AND CAPTURED

Shorty Tubbottom was concerned. He had not heard one word from any of the reward contestants since the cookout. Certainly he would have heard if they had caught the Bigfoot. His mom badgered him to go and find out since she was anxious to get this project done. All of her money was tied up in this costly money pit. Beside, Momma Tubbottom wanted to wear a crown and ride in the celebratory parade. Shorty was sure that this weekend would bring Squatch down from the hill and into his Bigfoot Habitat.

With darkness descending, Shorty decided to drive up the mountain and see what was going on. He dressed in black and laced his black boots, with inserts, to make sure he appeared taller than he actually was. Who knows? He may run into Bigfoot up there. He tucked a large flashlight in his waistband and jumped into his jeep. Up the hill he went, slowly. He knew exactly where to find the group of hunters. According to Andrew and his map, they would be right at Missing Toe Lane and just beyond, up to the Mountain Laurel marker. He stopped before they could hear his jeep and continued the trek up the mountain by foot.

Everything was quiet as he made his way up the arid road. If he remembered correctly, it had been weeks since the last rain. Suddenly, he heard knocking. *OH NO!* He stood still, listening intently. There it was again. Tree knocking. He knew that Bigfoot would knock on trees to communicate with others. Then, in the dry stillness, came a blood curdling scream. Shorty crept quickly into the nearby bushes and backed his way in deeper, just to make sure that not even Bigfoot would find him. Little did he know, with each tiptoe, that he was closing the only escape route the further he moved backwards. The entrance dwindled in size, each step triggering the closure. Before he knew it, he was locked in Bubba's Pull-TightBag.

Holy shamoly! He started to shout but then realized he may only attract Bigfoot. Something in there smelled awful. He used his flashlight and found the dead critter used for bait. He tried to find a way out but he was completely enclosed, sacked in with the stench. He started talking to himself. *Well, Momma. I didn't think I needed a knife or a weapon. I thought I was only going to check things out, to find out if any of the hunters heard, saw or trapped anything. I KNOW I am in one of their traps!! YOU DON'T HAVE TO REMIND ME!*

"Momma" he whimpered as he hunkered down on the floor of his encapsulated coffin. She was always there for him but not now. Alone, he resigned himself to wait until morning.

The knocking and the screams moved further away from him. For a moment, he thought he heard clackers but then realized he was probably dreaming. Hours later, in the pitch black, he let himself drift off.

Denise thought she heard screaming but decided she was dreaming. She was dreaming of her dad and how he always took good care of her. She wished that he was with her now. In the dream, she was crying, maybe even screaming, her arms outstretched, wanting her dad to come for her. She felt his arms around her and he rocked her back and forth. But there was a terrible smell. Her nostrils burned from the odor. As she was coming out of her sleep, she could swear that the RV was rocking. She tried to force herself back into the comforting dream. She wanted to tell her dad about her fall and how her bones and muscles ached. But it was useless. She couldn't return to sleep. She sat up and listened. The night was quiet except far away she could hear the clickety clack of the clackers. She was going to give Andrew what-for in the morning. He must have found his clackers. Denise would have sworn that Rhonda stole, and probably destroyed, those clackers.

Clickety clack. Clickety clack. *What is he thinking, using that thing in the middle of the night?* Denise turned over and pulled the blanket up over her head.

Clive, Clarice and Matthew continued up the mountain, knocking on trees and giving Bigfoot yelps and screams. So far, their attempts went without acknowledgment. The croaking of frogs was about the only noise in the forest. Occasionally, there would be crunching in the underbrush and they would spotlight a family of raccoons or opossums scrounging the barren landscape for bugs or berries. The night air was dry, the night sky dark and clear.

"I would love to see some clouds in the morning." Matthew spoke softly.

"Yeah. It is unbelievably dry." Clive responded.

"Yep, bone-dry. Some rain water would taste good right about now." Clarice groaned, rubbing the back of her grungy neck.

They worked their way back to the road, stopping to listen. They felt as if they were the only ones on this mountain. If only!

Noisily, Andrew caught up with them and was ranting and raving about the professors screwing with his traps. He was headed to the stream to see if any of his slap ankle bracelets had been disturbed.

"I'll be damned if a bunch of whiney women are going to cost me the reward!" He scuttled off toward the creek. "Why are there a bunch of floozies out here in the middle of the woods anyway? I don't have time for their shenanigans!" His voice descended into the dark timber, his flashlight fading into the night.

"Oh, hell no. We can't let him win that reward." Clive looked at Clarice. Clarice hurled out another blood curdling call. Although her mind would not let her believe, without seeing Bigfoot, she sure could scream like one.

Several deer lit up the night vision goggles. Franklin, Bubba and Jimbo knew that if there were deer around, then there was food for Bigfoot. "If I were Bigfoot, I'd be camping at the creek right about now. Everything's so parched." Bubba knew what critters would do; head to the water.

"Yes, that's where Bigfoot could find every thirsting creature, lapping up that cool, clear mountain water." At least there was a little breeze that helped keep the heat down but the descending leaves reminded him of fall. Even the early mornings had been clear, without a hint of mist. That was an unusual occurrence for this area. Now, the night air helped to calm down the lingering anxiety that Jimbo was feeling. He thought the area was too dry and in need of a big storm. Storms brings lightning, which is not good since they were surrounded by kindling.

Andrew tended to his traps and then slipped away into the forest. Heading north, he happened upon Franklin's zip line. He inspected it, thinking he might give it a go. Then he thought better. He walked towards the camp but thought how wonderfully fun it would be to go sailing in the hot air tonight. He doubled back to the zip line.

He used his flashlight to see the end of the line. Then he stood in complete darkness, listening. It would not be wise to be caught on the zip line by his competitors or by Bigfoot. He climbed the tree and sat on the platform. *What would make this a trap? It's clear all the way to the end.* Again, he sat in darkness and listened. Was he scared of the zip line or just anxious about getting caught? *Oh, to heck with it!*

Andrew harnessed up. *There ain't nobody around for miles. I might as well enjoy myself!* And with that, he flew down the hillside. He actually caught himself laughing, something he hadn't done in a very long time. He was moving a lot faster than he thought, and the end of the zip line was looming near. But, before he could get to the end, there was a snap. Suddenly he was jolted to a stop, mid-flight. His body rocked violently, the harness going from under his butt to under his knees. It tightened instantly. He was locked against the zip line, his knees having the only contact. Dangling high off the ground, Andrew kicked and tried to free himself but it was no use. He was captured for sure. It was like a huge zip tie locked his knees to the line and it was too strong to break. Using his ab muscles, he pulled himself up and wrapped his arm around the zip line. Then he urgently fumbled in his pockets for the radio but the radio was on the ground below him.

Clive, Clarice and Matthew made it back to camp and were surprised that Andrew was not there. They pulled out their sleeping bags and settled down to get some rest. The campfire had been put out some time earlier but it still smoldered. Clarice got up and poured a canteen of water on it, just to make sure. In the distance, she thought she heard yelling, so she stopped and stood still. Nothing. It was just her imagination. It was time to get some shuteye.

Franklin, Bubba and Jimbo decided to camp near the creek. Even if they couldn't catch Bigfoot in their traps, maybe Bubba would capture a photo of the big bipedal creature slurping up clear, cool water. With camera in one hand and a flashlight in the other, Bubba's dreamy thoughts soon floated away, down the mountain, along with the current of the nearby stream.

Chapter 14
Anger Builds

Monday morning arrived and the sun was extraordinarily hot and bright. There was no moisture in the air to buffer the searing rays. Clive rushed back to the camp to wake everyone. It was first light and he was already sweating.

"I need all the help I can get!" he declared as he prodded everyone awake. "Bring your bear spray and help me get an angry bear out of the hammock before he tears it to shreds!" No telling how long the bear had been trapped. Clive was disappointed that he did not have a Bigfoot captured in his hammock and he was beginning to think there was no Bigfoot on this mountain after all. *Why would Shorty Tubbottom waste all this money, time and effort if there was no Bigfoot? Maybe he's just off his rocker.* Clive led the way to the hammock.

Rhonda could hear someone yelling far away. She thought she was hallucinating from the crash or the sedative. She lay still, her head pounding, her body aching from head to toe. There it was again; a distant yelp of some kind. She sat up. It took every ounce of energy to do that.

"Denise! Lulu! Someone is yelling!"

Lulu popped her head in the narrow room where Rhonda was sitting on the edge of the bed. "Oh MY GOD! What happened to you, Lulu? Your face looks like you have chicken pox!"

"Yes, good morning to you, too." Lulu sat down next to Rhonda. She didn't feel so hot either. "I had a fall yesterday. My face decided to ski down the mountain side! There are tiny rocks embedded in each pore!" Lulu had to stop herself from crying. Rhonda looked at her with bewilderment as Denise hobbled in to see what was going on.

"My butt hurts so bad! My thighs are killing me!" Denise exclaimed as she made her way to sit down next to Lulu. "I landed on my feet but then somersaulted half way down the mountain. This hill is rocky. My thighs are bruised. My arms are bruised. My head is... Is my head still here?" Her gaze was blank until she spied Lulu's pockmarked face. "Oh my GOD, Lulu! Look at you!" Denise exclaimed.

All three were in bad shape. Rhonda had been only aware of her

58

own problems, not those of Denise or Lulu. Rhonda felt hers was the worst, of course. She was about to instruct Lulu and Denise on how to better take care of her when they heard a cry from the forest. They quieted. Again, they heard a cry. It sounded like an injured calf. Had any of them ever heard a calf?

"Okay, which of us is going to be *able* to go get help?" Rhonda asked, knowing full well it wasn't her. Denise offered to go to camp. "But it won't be quick!" she pronounced.

"See if anyone has any more sedatives while you're at it." Rhonda ordered as she settle back into the bed.

"It hurts to frown." Lulu stated as she made her way to the bathroom mirror. A half-hearted scream escaped her lips as she caught the first glimpse of herself. Even opening her mouth was painful. The skin was scraped off the full length of her nose. Her chin was clear of skin, too. They looked burned. Her forehead and cheekbones were clad with tiny particles of rock and dirt and were already festered with angry redness.

There was a knock at the door. Lulu slowly made her way to answer it. Franklin tried to hide his horror as he half-smiled at Lulu.

"Come on in. Rhonda is back there." She motioned as little as possible.

"Thanks." He brushed past her and made his way to the back of the camper, thinking Rhonda would be ingratiated for his help and kindness.

"Wow. You look horrible." He was shocked at how much black and blue there was and instantly regretted his choice of words.

"Greetings to you, too."

"I found your Timex." He held up Rhonda's watch, thinking she would be happy to see that it was intact.

"ROLEX." She stated through clenched teeth.

"What?" Franklin didn't know a Rolex from a Timex.

"ROLEX. ROLEX. ROLEX!" He thought Rhonda's eyes were going to pop out of her head, as they bulged bigger with each syllable she hissed.

Rhonda rubbed her head and wondered how she ever got here. *How stupid! How idiotic! How did she ever think she would EVER be around such IDIOTS!* Her head was pounding with anger. Anger at herself and anyone else within a mountain mile!

"Kitchi Sabe" was all Franklin could think to say. "Kitchi Sabe" was a song about a mythical giant, a symbol of honesty, respect and integrity.

She looked at him like he was crazy but he had felt the same when she was croaking, "Rolex. Rolex. Rolex." This showed that they lived on totally different mountains. That confusing moment brought instant clarity to Franklin, that he needed to be focused on, right now, right this very second, the reward and Bigfoot, and NOT Rhonda.

He was ready to get out of there. Softly, Franklin asked, "sedative?"

"Yes, please."

He fetched a sedative for Rhonda but that was the end of his thinking about her. He had the mighty Bigfoot and the mighty reward to go after and that was all that mattered. He didn't go back in the camper. He handed the sleeping pill to Lulu and watched as she closed the door. *That is how it should be, he thought to himself. I am just a mountain man and always will be. Ain't no use to think that Professor Rolex is interested in a simple man such as me.*

Franklin went to check the zip line and was ready to move it up the mountain. He kicked the loose pebbles along the dusty road. *I gotta quit thinking about that glorious face when Rhonda looked back at me while zipping down the hill. It was the happiest face I have ever seen.*

He slapped the side of his head, trying to force her out of his mind.

Franklin stopped in his tracks. He couldn't believe his eyes. Down the zip line, almost to the end, and hanging on for dear life, Andrew was crying. Franklin scurried up the tree and chopped the tie that held the branch that held Andrew tight in place. Andrew dropped like a sack of potatoes to the ground, hitting hard. He was too numb to feel anything. He sat for a long time, knowing he didn't have any feelings in his legs and wondered if he would ever feel them again. Andrew rolled to his side and tried to stand up. Franklin went to help but Andrew waved him off. Angry and frustrated, Franklin had no problem leaving him there. Neither man spoke, but Franklin was steaming. Andrew had screwed up his chance to catch Bigfoot. Franklin was so mad, he could choke Andrew's scrawny, arrogant neck. He wanted to slam him, hard, against the ground, again and again and again. *Who does he think he is?*

CHAPTER 15
ANGER ABOUNDS

Lulu gave the sedative to Rhonda. While waiting for Rhonda to drift off, Lulu heard a low, pitiful calling again. Denise had not returned, so she dressed and went to find Jimbo. He would know what to do. She explained to him the sounds they were hearing, coming from the forest. She needed his help. Besides, she didn't want to be wandering around alone, with the strange noises coming from the hill. Also, she couldn't run if something got after her.

Jimbo was getting ready to go and check his Big Pipe but went instead with Lulu to find out what she was talking about. Following the noise, they could hear a low whimpering with an occasional bellow. Their ears led them to the area of Bubba's PullTightBag. Since Bubba was off with Clive, releasing the hammock bear, Jimbo tried to figure out Bubba's contraption, all the while, thinking there was a large creature inside it. Maybe a wild hog, even a coyote or a bobcat, so he proceeded with caution. As he instructed Lulu to get behind the closest tree, he heard a small voice coming from inside the PullTightBag.

"Momma? Help me. Momma…" came a whimpering plea.

Jimbo thought there was a child inside. Without hesitation, he pulled out his hunting knife, pushed the limbs and branches aside and sliced into the macrame Bag, only to find Shorty Tubbottom. He was delirious, as Shorty grabbed Jimbo, calling him Momma. The stench took Jimbo's breath away. He dragged Shorty to a nearby tree and leaned him up against it.

"You get the reward for saving my life." Shorty hugged Jimbo's legs and would not let go.

Jimbo asked Shorty how he got up the mountain. Then, he helped Shorty back to his jeep. He told Lulu that he would drive Shorty back down the mountain and get a ride back up. He would check on the girls later, after he checked his Big Pipe, hoping he caught Bigfoot. Lulu was excited for him already getting the reward.

"No. Shorty didn't mean that. He's tired and exhausted. He still expects a Bigfoot, so we need to deliver." Lulu frowned. OUCH! She was more than ready to go home.

Franklin was fiercely troubled by Andrew's sabotage of his zip-line. There was no one to report this to and no penalty for what he did. Franklin decided to go after Andrew's traps, wherever they were, and destroy his chances of winning the reward. He knew Andrew spent time at the stream, so he headed there to snoop around, before Andrew could get any feelings back in his legs. He wandered up and down the creek bed, looking for Andrew's traps.

Meanwhile, Jimbo was going to have to explain to Bubba why he sliced up the PullTightBag. It was not on purpose and he thought there was a kid in the Bag, calling for his mother. It sure sounded pathetic and disturbing. Shorty Tubbottom should pay Bubba for the destruction, since he was snooping around in the dark. Bubba was out a night's chance to capture Bigfoot and would not be able to trap this evening either. "Man Oh Man! Bubba is going to be fit to be tied!" he thought.

In camp, Franklin paced back and forth angrily. Bubba was upset, too, when he found out about his PullTightBag. Andrew sat in a crumpled heap on the side of the campsite. Were the guys trying to sabotage each other, to destroy the chances of anyone catching Bigfoot? Clive's hammock was pretty much ruined. He didn't know if he would be able to make repairs in time for tonight's hunt. And now they find out that Shorty Tubbottom was out interfering.

"And," Matthew threw a fierce glance at Andrew. "Andrew or Shorty should be responsible for the destruction of my net gun!" Matthew moved towards Andrew with fists balled. Clarice and Clive stopped him.

"I don't know what y'all are complaining about! There was a whole family of raccoons asleep in the Castle Tent! They must have had a pillow fight because stuffing was everywhere, inside and out!" Clarice ranted.

"Well, what do you expect?" Clive snarled. "You led them right to it with that kitty food!"

Clarice was surprised at Clive. He was trying to look down his nose at her. This was difficult because she was a good six inches taller. *The nerve!*

Just then Andrew piped up.

"What the hell is wrong with your zip line? Are you trying to kill people!?!" shrieked Andrew.

Franklin squared off with Andrew, although Andrew was prone on the ground.

"I adjusted the angle of the zip line *according* to the weight of the Beast, so that it would speed up or slow down, *according* to mass. That was the only way the harness would suddenly rebound and trap him around the knees. Speed and weight are everything!" he snarled at Andrew. "But I didn't know I was dealing with a lowdown, sneaking, *skinny* jackass!"

"Alright guys," Clarice stepped in. "Let's decide about tonight. Where do we stand? I can still move the Castle tent and pray that Bigfoot will find it tonight." She gestured to Franklin. "You can still move the zip line up the mountain." Then she looked at Jimbo and asked, "Did you check your trap yet? Will you be ready to move up the mountain?" Jimbo nodded. Clive didn't know if the hammock could be used but was heading back, now that the bear was gone, to check it out. Andrew realized that all eyes were on him now. From the ground, he motioned that he was just fine and would be moving his traps as well. He would need all day to get his traps moved, especially in his shape. Somehow, he knew there would be no offers of help. They all agreed to meet later, back at the new camp further up the mountain. Everyone dispersed. Andrew tried to clean up the camp and pack up his supplies. An angry Franklin made plans to follow him later.

One more night. That was all they had left to capture Bigfoot. Matthew's net gun was still in working order. Apparently nothing tall had set it off last night. Once he moved it up to the next spot, he was going to make sure that no one, except Bigfoot, came near his net gun trap. He planned on sitting on a tree limb above the gun, to guard it and to be there when the capture happened. He just had to find the right spot, build a makeshift platform in the tree, calibrate his net gun, and then wait for nightfall.

Not only was the extreme heat and dryness adding to the angst and annoyance, but all of the hunters felt like they were chasing their tails. No one knew for sure, not even Shorty Tubbottom, if there was a Bigfoot to be found. And Shorty Tubbottom couldn't trust his own spy, since he was not forthcoming with any valuable information.

All the hunters came with original ideas and with high hopes but so far, most of their dreams had been dashed. It was not fun anymore. All bets were off. The only thing they could all agree on was making sure that the lowdown Andrew did not capture the reward.

The professors had not been able to do the research they had planned to do. Rhonda wanted to prove, beyond a shadow of a doubt, about the "Big

Fantasy," but a true scientist cannot prove that something does not exist. However, she could very well write about the true idiocy of men. The other two professors had hoped to learn about the habitat and means by which Bigfoot managed to not only survive but thrive in the beautiful scenic mountain paradise. Could it be a hoax? All were there to discover a Bigfoot that may not even exist, at least not on this mountain.

The caravan of hunters moved upward for their last night.

CHAPTER 16
A PHONY APOLOGY?

Franklin quickly moved his zip line up the mountain. He was so angry that he really didn't pay attention to what he was doing. In a blind rage, he was ratcheting, tightening, hammering and cursing. He had to find a way to get back at Andrew, to make sure he didn't capture Bigfoot and the reward. At least he wasn't thinking about the divine face of Rhonda. Gosh, she is extremely beautiful when she smiles. He wanted to see that laughing face again and again. STOP IT! Now he was cursing himself for thinking about her.

Obviously, no one cared about Andrew and his traps. He had been such a butt. Franklin had moved his zip line, along with Jimbo and his Big Pipe, and Matthew with his net gun. Clive set up his hammock but was not sure if it was strong enough to hold Bigfoot. Clarice had spent extra time setting up the Castle Tent, with additional rope and drawstrings underneath the whole spread. She wanted to make sure she had tried everything and had put her best foot forward during this whole adventure. She was confident Bigfoot was messing with her tent and she knew, for sure, she could use the million dollar reward.

Andrew was at the new campsite when everyone returned to rest for a while during the afternoon. It was a hopeless goal. They were all on edge, not knowing who to trust, wondering if one of them had been sabotaging the rest.

Andrew announced he was out of the game, not being able to fully move. He apologized to everyone. They were all in shock. Or maybe this was a ploy? They all cast him a sideways glance. Humble Andrew? Nahhhh.

"Alright. Alright. I know I have been a giant pain in the butt. I thought I had to keep all of you from winning the money by being aggressive. I had a lapse in judgment about the zip line. But I gotta tell you, it felt good! It felt like freedom, if only for a minute. It felt good to laugh!" Andrew was astonished to relive the joy of that ride. For him, that joy was bigger than Bigfoot. He actually mustered up a smile.

They all looked at each other, surprised, but still cautious of Andrew's intentions.

"I don't blame y'all. Not one bit. But I've decided I have a new calling. I'm gonna find me a piece of land with strong, beautiful trees and I'm gonna set up a commercial zip line, where everyone can come and zip for the love of zipping. It is such a joy, I just wanna share it." Andrew managed to get on his legs, although they were wobbly and weak.

"Last night, hanging from the zip line was a curse and a blessing. I found my way back to my heart, my joy."

He continued, "I had a lot of time to think, just hanging there and not knowing what was going to happen to me. Bigfoot could have torn me to shreds, if he had found me there. I could've lost both my legs. I spent the first couple hours, hanging there and cursing all of you. But then I realized I did it to myself. A million dollars wouldn't have saved me."

With fake enthusiasm, he continued, "So I let it go and I wish all of you the best of luck. I'm gonna beg the professors for a ride down the mountain tomorrow."

With that, Andrew hobbled away from camp.

As nightfall approached, the rest of the group decided to move up the mountain, closer to their traps. They still didn't trust Andrew. They wished each other luck, knowing tonight was the night: the last opportunity to nab the giant ape man. The mountain was getting smaller and smaller the closer they got to the top. They felt like they had managed to keep pushing Bigfoot further up the mountain. Tonight would be the downfall of the colossal cryptid.

There was tension in the stifling air. Stifling was a good word. Maybe they had been stifling each other, wanting to win at all costs. Maybe they still had a fight on their hands, with each other. Shorty and Andrew had sabotaged some of their traps. Knowing or unknowingly? That was the question. And that question helped raise the tension, for no one knew who they could trust. Maybe Shorty threw the professors in as spies or disruptors. Maybe Andrew was feeding them a line of bull about changing his life; maybe he hadn't changed at all, and was still going for the gold, no matter what it took.

Rhonda was still capable of ordering the other women around.

"Okay girls, this is our last night here. Y'all might as well start packing your stuff. As soon as the sun peeps over the horizon, I am driving this jalopy down the mountain. After we leave this compound, I'm going to stop at the first restaurant we come to and I am going to stuff myself. Then I am going to get myself home as quickly as possible, to wash this whole fiasco from my mind and body forever! I can't wait to sleep in my own bed." Denise and Lulu nodded. None of them felt well. It had been a rough weekend for sure.

Lulu brought damp washcloths to Rhonda. Rhonda wiped down her arms and legs and the core of her body. The slight chill of the damp cloths brought relief on this warm evening. It made her think of how Franklin had put warm washcloths on her bruised body, gentle and soothing, after her collision with the tree. No man had ever taken care of her before. She closed her eyes and thought of Franklin. He was a nice, gentle, kind man. She shouldn't have been so short with him.

Lulu showered as best she could without letting the spray hit her face. She would have to see a doctor as soon as possible. Her nose and chin were blistered. Tiny stones were still lodged in her cheeks. Jimbo had tried to help but he was scared of hurting her. She dressed and just as she was about to go find Jimbo, Andrew knocked on the door of the camper. Denise was immediately at her side, ready to crown him if he stepped foot near Lulu.

Andrew produced a small metallic sandal but Lulu didn't blink. She stared at him. He hung his head. He had been so hateful before.

"I think this must belong to one of you three ladies."

"Ya think?" Denise was being snotty but not admitting anything.

"I just wanted to return it to whomever and I wanted to apologize for being rude the other day. You may not know this, but I spent last night tied up on the zip line. I had many hours to think about my life. I know I have made a lot of mistakes. Just wanted to say I am sorry." He turned to hobble away.

"Wait." Lulu said, "I don't imagine there are too many around who will offer you any help and we can barely take care of ourselves."
Denise poked Lulu in the ribs. Lulu winced, but continued. "This thing has wheels. I think we can help you get your gear and take you up the mountain for the last night here."

Andrew tried to bow to the ladies but ended up toppling to the ground. Lulu and Denise went to his aid but the three of them were practically useless: bruised, sore, and lame. After managing to climb aboard the rundown RV, all three sat down, to rest before doing anything else.

"My cart is at camp, although I think there is no one else remaining there. They've all moved up." Andrew welcomed the ride.

"We'll leave in a moment. Just let me check on Rhonda." Denise went to tell Rhonda what was going on. Daydreaming about Franklin, Rhonda waved Denise away with "whatever" coming from her lips.

With light fading, they claimed Andrew's cart with his meager belongings. Lulu drove the mammoth box-on-wheels slowly up the mountain and found a place to park near the new camp.

Franklin approached the camper and told the girls to drive the
camper on up, above the traps of the other hunters.

Lulu complied and continued the trek on up the big hill. Jimbo
stopped her and got on board the camper. He was surprised to see Andrew
inside with the girls.

Lulu pulled him aside. "I think this is best. We can keep an eye on
Andrew and make sure he doesn't sabotage any more traps."

"Good thinking." Jimbo smiled at the very smart woman. He gave
sleeping tabs to Lulu and said, "make sure he doesn't."

Jimbo felt empowered, knowing Andrew wasn't going to screw
with anyone else tonight. He left the camper a happy and hopeful man.

"How about a nice cup of hot chocolate?" Lulu offered Andrew.

CHAPTER 17
UP TO NO GOOD

Franklin caught up with Matthew and suggested that maybe, since Andrew was caught on his zip line, that it might have been Andrew that diced up Matthew's net gun trap. No matter what Andrew said earlier, about his change in attitude and his life-altering experience while hanging from the zip line, Franklin was sure he was lying.

"I just don't trust that guy." Matthew nodded in agreement.

Meanwhile, Andrew was not interested in a cup of hot chocolate. Lulu was disappointed but she was not about to give up. She realized that she would do anything to help Jimbo. Whoa. Was she falling for Jimbo? Maybe so but she would have to think about all that later. Right now, since the professors were out of luck when it came to research and her big dreams of discovering the "Lifestyles of the Hairy and Famous," Lulu could at least keep Andrew from destroying Jimbo's Big Pipe. Franklin still had his zip line, Clarice still had her Castle Tent, alluring to the female persuasion, and there was Matthew's Net Gun trap. Fewer traps. Fewer opportunities to capture the cryptid. Lulu decided she would set out a few snares to help with the hunt. Who knows, she might be the very one to capture the creature! Wouldn't that be a hoot?

Denise found Lulu out around the camper and she joined her to help create the snares. With Jimbo's help, they set up two rope snares, strong enough to lift Bigfoot off the ground, hanging by his ankle. While working together, Denise told them of the strong odor and the rocking of the RV the night before. Jimbo grew excited. He told them that Bigfoot has been known to rock parked cars, jostling sleepers inside, and for stinking to high heaven, an unmistakable smell of rot, urine and feces. Denise and Lulu decided they would throw a party, to draw Bigfoot near the RV again. Jimbo told them that he would be nearby, just in case the creature did come for a visit.

Lulu was hoping that was true, that Jimbo would be nearby. She wanted to know more about him, his background in association with the U.S.A. Professional Bigfoot Hunters and if he had a significant other waiting at home for him. She thought they might have a lot in common, especially with her background in biology of primates. Besides, she was beginning to enjoy the great outdoors, a world full of information she had previously denied herself. There was much to see, to do, to learn. Surprising herself, Lulu was now interested in replacing the sandals for some stylish, mind you, hiking boots.

Andrew had managed to set up a camp. He made a quick meal of sandwiches, chips, fruit cups and bottled water. There were protein bars, beef jerky and coffee. He settled down on his skimpy sleeping bag and waited for the others to show up. He knew no one was happy with him, or with Shorty Tubbottom, after what happened last night. For the moment, he would try to stay in the background. His thoughts turned to the million dollar reward. That would be a handsome sum to buy and build a business of his own. He wasn't concerned about Clive's hammock. He had heard Clive ranting about the bear damage. He also knew Bubba's PullTightBag was destroyed. *Let's see…who else do I have to worry about? Hmmm…Jimbo's Big Pipe might be a problem, but right now, I gotta get to the stream and set up those slap ankle bracelets!* When the others began to arrive at camp, Andrew stood as best he could and then hobbled off. He had found a strong limb, tall enough to lean upon, as he favored one leg over the other. He was actually feeling stronger, but no one needed to know that.

Jimbo, Lulu and Denise brought Rhonda a sandwich and a fruit cup from the camp. She sat up in the bed and ate, questioning what everyone had been up to. Rhonda looked a little better. She thought a couple of her toes were broken. She had tried to stop her crash, using her feet and hands but her knees and ribs felt the most pain. Lulu's face didn't look much better but she had kept herself busy, trying not to think about it. And Denise's bruises were turning from purple and blue to yellow and green.

Lulu explained to Jimbo that her offers of something to drink for Andrew were refused. "He was polite and seemed appreciative but he didn't stick around for long." Jimbo smiled at her and suggested, "He's up to something, I can guarantee it." With that, Jimbo left the camper and headed for the stream, to see if he could spy on Andrew.

Opening the cargo bay on the camper, Lulu pulled out the amplifier and the music player. She hooked it all together and adjusted the volume. With nightfall, she and Denise planned on drinking wine and dancing, thinking Bigfoot might be interested in their antics. They didn't mention a thing to the "Rototiller," knowing full well she would club them for even thinking Bigfoot would come a-calling.

CHAPTER 18
WHERE IS CLARICE?

In the heat of late afternoon, the stream was a beautiful sight, as the clear running water splashed and frolicked over the rocks. Some of the rocks were huge. Along the bank, boulders nestled into the soft mud. Jimbo pretended to be sightseeing just in case someone was watching. He meandered along the stream until he found who he was looking for. It wasn't Andrew, though. It was Franklin. He witnessed Franklin ripping the slap ankle bracelets clear out of the mud and tossing them up into the timberline, chain and all. His fury was powerful and strong. Then, with Jimbo approaching, Franklin seemed to simmer down. They sat on a boulder and talked about what had just happened. Franklin said he wasn't sorry. Andrew had screwed him from catching Bigfoot last night and now it was Andrew who needed to suffer. Jimbo agreed. They jumped from boulder to boulder and eventually made their way back up to the road. They would find Bubba and then all three would shadow Andrew for the rest of the night.

The dusty road released little wisps of dirt that billowed up with each step.

"Seems way too dry." Jimbo was still worried about the parched landscape.

As they searched for Bubba, Franklin said, "This dry climate is unusual. And look at that sky. Not a cloud anywhere in sight. We're gonna be able to touch the stars tonight!" Franklin was trying to lighten up. He had vented his anger on the traps by the stream and he was now feeling better about his chances with Bigfoot. The breeze picked up a bit and blew dry leaves from the trees to the ground. The canopy of trees shaded the whole road up the hill. The last bit of sunlight was dancing between branches. The sun would be down soon. Bubba found his way to Franklin and Jimbo and the three kicked pebbles up the powdery mountain road.

Matthew threw his pack on his back and scurried up the tree to the platform he had built earlier in the day. His net gun trap was not far away. He softly dropped the backpack on the platform and settled down for a quiet rest before it got dark. He rested his head on the backpack. The early evening sky was clear and bright. The air smelled of pine. He loved the sharp, fresh scent, for it meant peace and solitude. The forest was home to him. He feared nothing, not even Bigfoot. He was king when he was in the forest. As the sun set in the west, he heard music riding on the gentle breeze.

Rhonda was propped up in a chair near the camper. Franklin smiled at her. She smiled back. She was looking better to him. She didn't know the girls had set up rope snares on the backside of the camper. She didn't know the music could possibly entice Bigfoot. It never crossed her mind, of course, since there was no such thing.

"I think Bigfoot prefers country music instead of pop music." He teased her, listening to Jepsen's "Call Me Maybe."

"My music tastes are too sophisticated for Bigfoot and most everyone else around," she stated, preferring classical music. "I don't know how they came up with that stuff." She waved away the music as if to banish it from her world. Actually, she really didn't care about the music. Instead, she was feeling peacefully reflective. The world seemed so big, so undiscovered and she was feeling gratitude—*yes, Rhonda was feeling gratitude—for being a part of it.*

"The sun will be setting soon. Are you feeling the breeze?" He asked.

"I am feeling a bit cool."

He went in the camper and brought out a light blanket. He covered her. "Tuck. Tuck. Tuck." he said as he pretended to gently tuck the edges under her legs. She laughed. There. There it was. That shining face he had seen on the zip line. He was falling hard.

"Gotta go," he said regretfully and used long strides to catch up with Bubba and Jimbo going into the timberline. The hunt for Andrew was on.

Clive came around asking if anyone had seen Clarice. He was beginning to worry because he hadn't seen her all afternoon. He knew she was capable of being in the woods all by herself but she didn't show up at camp earlier in the day. There was one rule they had set for the group: to always check in at least once a day. Concerned, he went into the forest to find her.

Clarice was quiet as she thought about the group of hunters. She wondered why they didn't even consider that a female Bigfoot, if there was such a thing, would be highly interested in sparkly, shiny things. A decorated tent with twinkling lights…what SheFoot wouldn't be excited about looking inside? To see comfy pillows and blankets. What a treat to rest her tired head on such comfort. If he or she really existed. Clarice had searched high and low for years now. Not one Bigfoot hair. Not one Bigfoot carcass. Not one Bigfoot sighting. She didn't know whether to consider herself lucky or unfortunate. It was funny that she had picked out a pink princess tent, knowing she was not a girly girl herself. In her tomboyish ways, she preferred the relaxed style of comfort and ease. No time for hairstyles, heels, or high society.

Well, Clive's hammock is probably not in the running. And that net gun contraption was destroyed. And that silly PullTightBag idea was incredibly juvenile. I think I'll go and see what that Big Pipe is all about. It may not stand up to the test either. That would be great. Less traps means less hunters in the game. My castle tent may come out on top after all. She ventured off into the woods, baseball bat in hand. She might practice some screams, some tree knocking once it got dark.

After more than a few dead ends, she finally came upon the Big Pipe. It practically called out to her with its bright colors. She peered inside. She couldn't see how this was going to capture even a small, sightless mole. She stooped and stepped inside. It was quite smelly in there but she was used to the putrid smells of dead flesh. Near the center was a small table with a furry creature served up for dinner. She poked the tiny table with the wooden bat and with that, the table collapsed, dropping the dead fur-ball to the floor of the Pipe. Instantly, she was swept off her feet as the Big Pipe swung up off the ground and closed itself off at the top, the openings meeting together above her head. She was trapped in a giant hanging doughnut! "Well, whack a mole!" she cried out in frustration. "Shoot a monkey!" she wailed, shaking the narrow prison of metal rings.

Chapter 19
Caught Again

Clive thought he heard Clarice. He had been looking for her for quite some time now. He was also thinking of taking out the Big Pipe without getting caught. He moved in the direction of the swearing. The Big Pipe was hanging from a strong tall tree. It was sealed off, with the bulging body of Clarice inside at the bottom. She was cursing her own stupidity.

"Hellooo???" Clive teased her, knowing she didn't think there was a Bigfoot in existence. "Bigfoot, are you in there?" Clive knew it would irritate her to no end.

"Darn it, Clive! Help me outta here!" she bellowed.

"Hmm, I think you may have to stay in there until Jimbo lets you out!" He smiled to himself.

"I'm gonna kill you when I get outta here!" She couldn't stamp her feet because there was nothing but air below her. The whole contraption was only off the ground maybe ten or twelve inches but she couldn't know that.

Clive moved around the trap trying to figure out how it was made and how to release Clarice from it. He realized that there were metal rings keeping it tubular. Even if he cut the fabric, she wouldn't be able to slip between the metal rings. He was going to have to get above it and slice the rope that was holding it up. That meant shimmying up the tree, which he hated. It is a lot harder to do, with bare hands and no equipment. He had better hurry or they would both be caught screwing with Jimbo's Big Pipe trap.

"Hold on inside there. I gotta get up the tree and cut this rope. You'll drop about ten inches or so. Just be prepared."

"Well, stop talking and just do it!" she ordered.

"Hey, I can leave you here for Jimbo to find you. He won't be as nice!"

"Sorry." She realized she literally didn't have a leg to stand on.

Whoosh. The whole thing dropped to the ground. Clive quickly climbed down and released the snared rope at the top, opening the doughnut and helping Clarice out.

"Let's get out of here NOW!"

They hurried into the forest, away from the scene of the damaged doughnut. It would be hell to pay when Jimbo found out about this, his missed opportunity to capture Bigfoot and the reward. They headed for camp that was near the Path of the Yeti marker. In the dark, they passed the camper, just north of the marker, but didn't stop to congregate with the others. The music was blaring Swift's "Cruel Summer" and the Professors were huddled together, gossiping about something. Clarice and Clive would circle around and approach the RV from the south, making it appear they were hunting below the rest. It would look too suspicious if they came running from the North.

Startled, Clarice realized that she had left the bat in the Big Pipe. She was so anxious to get out, she had forgotten it. She whispered her dilemma to Clive. Clive decided he would go back and retrieve it. He could move quicker if she wasn't with him. He quickly circled back into the woods.

Andrew hobbled to the sight of the mangled Big Pipe. He lifted one end and looked inside. Strange. He didn't see how this would ever work. After surveying the cut rope and the severed doughnut ends, he realized there was an object inside it. He fished around until he found a way to pull the wooden bat to him. *Hmm. Wonder who's been up to no good.* He swung the bat over his shoulder and grabbed his support stick. He limped his way back into the woods. But not before he was spied by Bubba and Franklin. Just then, Clive ran up on both of them. Franklin told him that it looked like Andrew had destroyed another trap and that he used a bat. Clive didn't correct them. Then they thought to question Clive why was he there? He told them that he was still looking for Clarice and asked if they had seen her. They shook their heads and watched Clive head for the dry road. They decided they had better get back to camp, too.

The wind was picking up. It was strange that the wind was coming from the south, breezing through the trees as Clive headed down the hill to the camp. It felt good to him. And it felt good that he didn't get caught retrieving Clarice's bat.

On his little platform above his net gun, Matthew saw the stars come out, one by one. He thought about his favorite uncle who used a telescope to identify the constellations. He taught Matthew all about the stars. He fell asleep, counting each of them.

Franklin and Bubba made it back to camp. As the music blared, they wondered where Andrew had gotten off to but decided to check on the ladies. "They may be dancing." Bubba was hopeful.

At the camper, Franklin dropped to the ground near Rhonda. Denise and Lulu were dancing together to Bruno Mars' "Just The Way You Are." There was a sudden gust of wind, sending dead leaves swirling across the open, baked road. As the music blared, there came a terrifying scream from behind the camper. Franklin and Bubba looked at each other and grabbed their flashlights. Neither wanted to go first, so they both stepped together gingerly to the end of the camper and slowly peeked around it.

Suspended in air, there was Andrew, hanging upside down and flailing about. Clive and Clarice, just returning to camp, came running to see what was the matter. Jimbo kept Lulu behind him, in case something came running towards them out of the dark.

Franklin and Bubba started laughing. It served Andrew right to get caught up in one of the girls' snares. Finding it hilarious, Franklin bellowed, "And he thought they would never catch anything!"

"Dang you all! Get me down from here!" Andrew was spitting his anger everywhere!

"Maybe that is the safest place to keep you—safe for the rest of us!" Franklin couldn't stop laughing, as Bubba gave him a high five.

Clarice stepped forward and warned them that it wasn't good for his blood pressure to keep him upside down like that. She suggested they help him down. Otherwise, they may have to care for him until all of this was done. No one wanted to do that.

Clive shimmied up another tree and was surprised by the sudden and erratic wind that was kicking the branches around. He spotted a mass of clouds descending the very spot where they were congregating. The electrified clouds were blinding yet quiet on their approach. He used his knife to cut Andrew free. He sure hated to do it, thinking Andrew should stay tied up until the hunt was over. As if in concert, just as Andrew pelted the ground...KaBOOM! Lightning struck a nearby tree.

KaBOOM! The next strike was even closer! There was strong, clamorous thunder but no rain.

"Where did all the clouds come from? Holy Cow! A storm is coming!" Matthew instructed the ladies to get in the camper and to stay there. In an instant, he smelled smoke.

"Oh My God! FIRE!" He yelled to the others.

Then they all smelled smoke and knew this was not good.

Before they could gather up the amplifier, the music equipment, the chairs, the blankets, the food, they spotted flames spreading rapidly on the hill below them. Clive realized that the gusty wind was pushing the fire to the North. And it was quickly spreading. The earth was so dry, it was perfect tinder. Without hesitation, they all piled into the ancient camper. But was everyone there? Maybe they had better move above the fire and go down the other side of the mountain. They were all peering out the large windshield. Franklin started the camper and floored it but the camper did not respond right away. With a jolt, it lurched forward, groaning, leaping now into action, throwing everyone toward the back of the motor home.

He drove to the top of the mountain. The camper chugged its way up, in no hurry to go anywhere. The fuel gauge had no needle reading, so Franklin couldn't tell if there was enough gas to get them down the mountain. At BigFeet Peak (that's what Grandpa Tubbottom called it), the men got out of the camper to survey the situation. The fire was spreading rapidly, totally ringing the mountainside, in every direction that they could see. They quickly debated and decided that they would have to drive down the mountain *through* the fire. They had no time to ponder their options.

CHAPTER 20
MISSING MATTHEW

Perched on the platform above his trap, Matthew was dreaming.

The red Lamborghini was oh, so responsive. Grasping the wheel, he delighted in having extreme speed and agile control as he raced along the road. Soon, he would pass the stands, with fans cheering him on. Clarice was there, smiling that glorious smile. He couldn't help but smile, too.

Loudly and without warning, the lightning struck close. It jarred Matthew off the platform. He noticed the net gun was spinning, which was odd. Barely awake, he landed on his feet, but more like a stumbling fall. Yet he caught himself before he got hurt. A yelp escaped him from deep within. Just as he gained his balance and stood upright, the net gun swung around and shot the rope net, which rapidly enveloped him in its web. He tried to free himself but it was impossible. The more he fought the more entangled he became.

He tried to calm himself, to think this through, knowing he could get himself out. He stopped and fished around for his pocketknife, then remembered he had zipped it into his backpack, which was still on the platform. He wouldn't be able to finagle his way back up the tree, not with this netting around him. He sat down and wondered if he should start yelling for help. It was at that moment that he smelled smoke. *Holy cow! Please don't let that be a forest fire. Maybe it is just the campfire I am smelling.* But he could see the flame-throwing clouds aiming for the top of the mountain. Like the red sports car, the fire was racing up the mountain.

Rhonda was worried. This did not look good. She looked at Lulu and Denise and thought about never seeing them again. Rhonda certainly surprised herself that she thought first of Denise and Lulu—not herself. *What if this was the end?* She refused to even acknowledge such a thought. She and the professors had much to prove yet. And what if she had just recently met a man, a real man, worth dating? Certainly, she had time to see how that would turn out?

Taking inventory, Clarice realized that Matthew was not with the group. The others reported they hadn't seen him and Clarice was instantly out of the camper. "We gotta find Matthew NOW!" She screamed to the others. They split up to hunt for him, hoping against all odds they would find him before the fire engulfed the whole mountain.

Momentarily, Rhonda had a quick guilty thought about leaving the idiot men behind. All she had to do was jump into the drivers' seat. But that meant leaving Franklin behind. Nope, her heart was now willing to take a chance. In that fiery moment, she saw Denise and Lulu in a new light as she looked at their frightened faces. They were now more than colleagues. They were friends. And Franklin was more than an idiot man to her. She would do whatever she could to get them down the mountain, to safety.

The sky was dark except for the lightning that exposed the heavy clouds hanging overhead. The billowing clouds held onto their content, angrily clashing into each other, sending out thunderous rumbles. Matthew yelled between the monstrous claps, hoping for help to soon arrive. The smoke was getting stronger and thicker and with that, he struggled, panicking to free himself, with no luck. His yells turned into urgent screaming. His eyes were burning and his breathing was getting shallow. He prayed it would rain. Anything to stop the fire and the smoke! He tried desperately to not let the smoke into his lungs. His throat was hoarse. "Tell me this ain't ironic" he spoke out loud. He tried to stand. "Caught by my own trap! HELP! HELP! HELP!" He increased the volume with each word. "CLIVE! CLARICE! I'M HERE!" He was going to keep yelling until his last breath.

The others met back up at the camper. Deciding to descend the mountain, the men walked alongside the camper as Denise drove slowly down the big hill, each man yelling Matthew's name. There was very little time left.

"STOP!" Jimbo yelled. "LISTEN! Over there. I think I heard Matthew calling!" He pointed to the blackness to his left, just before the Path of the Yeti marker. Below, he could see the fire moving their way. Denise tried to steer the camper's headlights in the direction Jimbo was headed. The smoke was beginning to hide everything from them.

Franklin, Jimbo and Clive ran toward the yelling.

"MATTHEW! MATTHEW!" They tried to get Matthew to respond again. Faintly, they could hear Matthew. They yelled again and again, with Matthew answering as best as he could. They flung their arms, trying to part the smoke in their path, to no avail. Clinging to each other's shirttails, they were almost ready to turn around and head back to the camper when suddenly, they were on top of Matthew.

They struggled to get him out of the net but couldn't. Frantic, they picked him up, net and all. At this point, Matthew didn't care if his backpack and his belongings were left behind. He didn't care if Bigfoot was ever caught. Matthew did not care, one iota, about a million dollars. He just wanted to breathe.

Coughing and sputtering, they struggled to get Matthew to their only hope—the suddenly beautiful, dented and ramshackle camper.

Bubba took the steering wheel, getting ready to gun it as soon as Matthew and the others were safe on board. Clarice, Rhonda, Lulu and Denise stayed huddled on the small couch extending back from the driver's seat. The smoke grew thicker by the minute. Remembering his trail safety training, Bubba started blowing the horn in a rhythmic pattern, so that the other four men would be able to find the camper. He closed off all the ventilation system, so as to not bring in the smoke. He was more than a little worried. It looked like a thick smoky fog was now their doom.

A tremendous banging at the side of the camper jolted them. The men lunged through the door with their hefty bundle. Franklin, Jimbo and Clive lay on the floor, coughing, while trying to free Matthew. Matthew was coughing uncontrollably while Clive cut away at the heavy netting, wondering how Matthew ever got all this in the net gun.

All of the hunters were finally together.

Andrew never lifted a finger to help. Maybe he was paralyzed by panic but he just sat in the passenger seat, quiet and dumbfounded. As soon as Franklin got up from the floor, he ordered Andrew to the back of the RV. Andrew complied.

Franklin told Bubba to drive down the mountain.

He jumped in the driver's seat, put it in gear and moved slowly along, in the dense smoke, not seeing any more than fifteen feet in front of the creeping vehicle. They were nearing the first burn line. He saw an opening in the fire line and rushed the tired camper through. Limbs came crashing down on the RV, some falling to the wayside. It looked like the whole world was ablaze. The limbs of the trees held fire all the way to their tips, finally breaking loose with the heat.

Lulu screamed with each limb that hit the rooftop. Denise held her close, covering her eyes. "Just don't look!" Denise instructed her. Rhonda held Denise and Lulu in a huge hug, silently praying they would make it out alive. The others stood, clinging to the cabinets and sink, trying to stay on their feet but feeling helpless in their situation. Matthew was sitting up, his back against the kitchen cabinet, while Andrew sat rigid, eyes closed, with his back against the door.

The damaged RV looped back, along the side of the burning mountain. There was another burn line to get through. Bubba closed his eyes and floored it, not knowing if he was still on the road or heading off the edge of the mountain.

"Jeez! I can't see a thing!" Franklin yelled. "Where was that dangerous curve that Shorty was talking about? I don't want you to drive off that ledge! This smoke is unbelievable!"

"Tell me about it!" Bubba responded, swiping the windshield with his hand, trying to clear his vision. Both were terrified. Suddenly lightning blinded them.

KaBoom! The RV rattled. Lulu screamed again.

Without missing a beat, the roaring clouds released their load. The heavens opened up and dumped a gully-washer of rain. The windshield wipers were unable to keep up. First, they couldn't see through the smoke and now they couldn't see with all the rain.

Suddenly, the camper slammed into huge boulders, stopping the vehicle dead in its tracks. The large wrench on the edge of the kitchen sink went sailing right into Andrew's big, arrogant head. Simultaneously, the violent force slammed everyone forward, right up to the massive front windshield. Just as abrupt as their stop and like divine intervention, there was a sudden clearing. In the headlights, they could see what appeared to be Bigfoot and an even smaller Bigfoot, fly from the roof of the camper and land in the shallow stream that flowed in front of them. With quick reflexes, the two creatures jumped to their feet and forcefully waded away, lumbering off into the darkness. The only sound the thunderstruck passengers could hear now was the clickity clack of the clackers that the larger Bigfoot grasped. They could also see a soggy pillow tucked under the right arm of the smaller Bigfoot, her bright pink beads bouncing around her neck.

With mouths open, no one uttered a word. No one moved. The RV groaned. The rain began to pick up again.

CHAPTER 21
HEADING HOME

The rain came fast and furious. The stream in front of them was quickly rising. All around the RV, the forest was steaming. They all checked on each other, to make sure no one was hurt. Mostly, all were dazed, unsure of what to do next.

Stumbling from the camper, the weary hunters began praising the rain. They were exuberant and happy to be alive. They were laughing at the sight of each other, all dirty and worn out. Even Andrew was smiling and twirling without his support staff.

They went slowly downhill, helping each other along the way. Bubba had the only flashlight and was the lead. He held Rhonda's hand as they slipped along the now muddy road.

Franklin addressed Andrew. "I see you are doing quite well without your stick, dancing wilder than anyone else."

Andrew stood tall and remarked, "If I hadn't had to contend with all of you, I woulda caught that Bigfoot!" They all groaned in unison.

"I think we saved Bigfoot AND AN IDIOT from the forest fire." Rhonda exclaimed.

Lulu and Denise were surprised by her declaration. Rhonda had seen Bigfoot and the "Light!"

Clive grasped Clarice's hand and danced her down the hill. They were exhilarated. Each and every one of them, because the outcome could have been so different.

Below the smoldering forest and not far down the road, the hunters were met by Rangers, who carted them down to the pavilion. Their only belongings were left behind in the camper. No sandals, no slinky vest or silk blouse was worth a life.

"Nothing matters." Rhonda stated, realizing that the people who surrounded her was all that mattered. "A million dollars wouldn't have helped us up there. But we were in this together. And we survived together! We made it!" She hugged Franklin with everything in her. She was not going to let this man walk out of her life.

The sun was close to coming up when they were met by Shorty

Tubbottom. He listened to all that they had endured and saw that they had become friends; not hunters, not rivalries, not acquaintances. They had become close to each other and grateful to be alive. He thanked them for participating and he offered them each a check to cover their loss of belongings and a little toward the future. But he was especially happy to know for sure that Bigfoot was on his mountain. "Did anyone happen to get a photo?" Bubba felt for the camera. It was still in his pocket.

The Rangers drove the hunters back toward civilization. Not caring how dirty they were, Rhonda instructed the driver to stop at the first restaurant they saw, no ifs, ands or buts. They were all famished, having not eaten a decent meal since the beginning of the hunt. Around the corner, they could see a rundown restaurant and a sign that read:

WELCOME TO BIGFOOT BURGERS!

What a beautiful sight! The rustic establishment was much like a smorgasbord restaurant, with a long buffet overflowing with lettuce, tomatoes, pickles, peppers, onions, cheeses and sauces. There was a heaping tray full of French fries and another with tater tots, alongside a bowl of potato salad large enough for Bigfoot. The spread reminded Rhonda of the first night at SquatchWatch Pavilion. But she needn't stuff her pockets or blouse this time. What she was taking with her now was more lasting: A permanent reminder that people are important in her life. She always thought she was alone in her battles "against the world." Friends, not frills, are more satisfying than food. She smiled at Franklin.

Speaking of stuffing, they all laughed as they stuffed their faces. Clive looked at Clarice and asked, "Do you believe in Bigfoot now?" She thought for a moment and said, "I can only surmise that I was delirious from panic, anxiety, fear and hunger!"

"But you saw Bigfoot! WE ALL DID!" he stammered.

Lulu looked at Rhonda, curious to know what she thought. "What do you think about Bigfoot now, Professor?"

Rhonda couldn't care less about Bigfoot. Or about proving its non-existence. One man filled her thoughts. Her next adventure would be to discover and capture his heart. She knew it was real. She hugged Lulu and said, "If that was Bigfoot that we saw, then Bigfoot is where he belongs—free and strong and thriving. We should all be so lucky."

THE END!